RAGE ON THE RANGE

A Terrence Corcoran Western

JOHNNY GUNN

WOLFPACK
PUBLISHING
— EST 2013 —

Rage On The Range
A Terrence Corcoran Western

Johnny Gunn

Kindle Edition
© Copyright 2018 Johnny Gunn

Wolfpack Publishing
6032 Wheat Penny Avenue
Las Vegas, NV 89122

ISBN: 978-1-64119-326-9

FOREWORD

This novel is based on an actual act of criminal behavior in which the criminal won the day. In the Soldier's Meadow area north of the Black Rock Desert, a squatter took some land and started raising cattle and a family. There was no school and the squatter hired a man to run his ranch while he took his family to a nearby community that had a school.

On returning, the hired man had brought friends with him and refused to give the ranch back to the squatter. There was no law in the area at that time and the squatter was driven off at gunpoint.

RAG

CHAPTER ONE

"I know my brand when I see it and those are my cattle in that sales pen. How did you get them? Why are they there?" Nathaniel Coppersmith, just turned thirty-five years a week ago, was - in turn - angry, mystified, and fearful seeing two hundred head of his cattle in a sales yard in Winnemucca, Nevada. "You know as well as I, Lefty Tom, those are my cattle. They're wearing my brand."

Lefty Tom Atkins owned the Humboldt Stockyards, one of the busiest along the western corridor of the intercontinental railroad, and he stood silent for a moment or two, shaking his head full of long curly hair, hat in hand. He pulled a rag from his pants pocket and wiped his face. "Fact is, Nate," he said as he took a deep breath and wiped his brow again, "that was your brand and those were your cattle. The man what drove those steers in had valid papers signed by Reg Chapman himself."

Chapman was the federal land agent for Humboldt County, the agent that handled all the federal Homestead Act legalities and other federal properties. He was known as a stickler for following the letter of the law to its final period.

"There ain't nothin' I can do, Nate. I know'd them was your beef when I saw the first one, but them papers told me different."

"Just who was it had those so called papers you're so willin' to believe?" Nate Coppersmith had his shoulders all bunched up, his fists of gnarled knuckles ready for action, and Lefty took a step back. Coppersmith homesteaded his one hundred sixty acres northwest of Winnemucca three years ago, built a nice home for he and his wife Susan, and was willing to spend the rest of his life on that high mountain desert land just a few miles south of the Oregon border.

Coppersmith was a big man who nobody could say ever threw his weight around. Well over six feet tall and about two hundred pounds, narrow at the hips and broad in the chest, the man loved weightlifting contests and got involved in boxing matches at the drop of a hat. There wasn't anyone in Humboldt County who could remember him throwing a punch in anger or threatening to draw a weapon. It just wasn't in him, most would say. But when Lefty Tom looked into his eyes at that moment, he wondered.

Those blazing eyes would skin a coyote with their heat and boil two rabbits on the side, Tom Atkins thought. He didn't want to tell Coppersmith the truth, and knew if he didn't and Nate found out he lied, he'd have to leave the county.

"Why, Curly Joe Simpson, of course. You gave up your homestead and he took it over is what Chapman told me."

The truth came as a flash of heat lightning almost driving Nate Coppersmith to his knees. All at once he understood and the understanding was terrifying. He needed more than a talk with agent Chapman; he needed to break out the Sharps rifle and Colt handguns. "My good friend, Curly Joe Simpson," he muttered. "My ranch foreman, Curly Joe." Coppersmith stood stock-still, slowly shaking his head from side to side.

Anger flashed through him like a rampaging torrent and he knew he had to take hold of it, keep his emotions under control, not go on a rage and tear out walls, destroy buildings, and kill Curly Joe Simpson. He had to control this rage, for Susan's sake, for the children. "Curly Joe Simpson; therefore, I'm responsible because it was I who brought him onto the ranch." He said that so softly that Lefty wasn't sure he really heard it.

Nate Coppersmith kicked some dust around, gave the herd of steers wearing his brand a long look, patted Lefty Tom on the shoulder, and walked slowly out of the stockyards. He mounted his horse and walked him back into town to the little home he rented for his family so his daughter could recuperate from a long illness. "This all started because I was willing to trust a man so I could make a better life for my wife and children," he muttered walking toward the small cabin south of the railroad tracks.

It was a fine spring morning just eighteen months ago when Curly Joe Simpson rode into the yard at the Sleepy U, a tired, dusty cowman looking for work. "Couldn't have picked a better time to show up, Simpson," Coppersmith said. "Not too many want to work this far out." Simpson had good names and places he talked about, seemed to know his business and Coppersmith put him to work.

"I tell you, Susan, this new man Simpson has two friends down in Austin who will come up if we need the hands. If we need the hands?" he laughed. "We have a fine new crop of calves and we need the hands. Old Dancing Antelope will sure be glad of the help."

Rocky Rockefeller and Slant Eyed Tom O'Neil rode up

from the Austin mines a few days later and were put to work right away. "They aren't really the cowmen they think they are, Susan, but we need the hands. Simpson can throw a fair rope and that feller they call Slant Eye rides well. They'll probably hustle out when that first winter storm hits."

Susan Coppersmith liked to feed the crew their morning and evening meals and the men ate well. "You fix a fine table, Mrs. Coppersmith," Curly Joe Simpson said. "Is your daughter not feeling well?"

Virginia, 'Ginny', six years old, was not a strong child and seemed to catch every germ that floated through northern Nevada. "She's getting stronger as she gets more age on her," Susan said.

That summer was hot and dry, and the small crew Nate Coppersmith had worked hard the whole time. As fall approached, the weather turned cold and wet and little Ginny seemed to suffer from constant ailments. "I would really like to spend this winter in Winnemucca, Nate. Ginny would be warm and dry. I know it would be a hardship but I don't think she will live through another winter here."

The idea of Susan and Ginny moving to town for the winter became kitchen table talk and Curly Joe Simpson made it bunkhouse talk with his compatriots as well. "This job has gotten us what I've been hopin' for. There's gotta be posters spread all over after those bank jobs in New Mexico and California. Hiding out here and getting paid, too," he laughed and said, "has been perfect and just got better.

"I have a plan that will make us a lot of money. You remember me telling you about that feller I met, the government big shot? Well, with a little help here and there, we're gonna own this place. We need to convince that big dumb rancher to go to Winnemucca with his wife and brat kid."

"Why?" Rockefeller was slow in everything he did including thinking.

"If he's off the ranch for a certain amount of time, we can claim he abandoned it and his homestead and file on it ourselves."

"That don't make no sense," Rockefeller said.

"It does if we turn right around and sell it," Slant Eyed Tom said. "Isn't that what brought us here in the first place?"

"Sure was. That letter I got when we were in Santa Fe." Simpson was a cock of the walk, dressed in the best he could buy and with the bank jobs in New Mexico and California, he bought a lot of fancy stuff. Many of his old gang wouldn't ride with him because he stuck out so. Every lawman had descriptions of the rooster.

"Think you can talk Coppersmith into that?" Slant Eyed Tom thought a ranch like this with a fine herd of beef would bring a good price. "It would mean spending the winter here but that's a cozy house and we'd have plenty of meat to eat."

"You boys back me up and we'll be the nicest men on the face of the earth and, yes, sir, we'll be more than happy to take care of your little old ranch and them cows and sheeps so you can keep your pretty girl well for the winter." Laughter could have been heard clear up at the ranch house if someone stood on the porch.

Susan was crying softly, sitting in a large overstuffed chair by the fireplace after Nate told her the sad tale of losing their homestead. "What will we do?" she finally asked.

"First, I'm going to call on Mr. Chapman at the land office and then I'm going to ride out to Seamus Doherty's ranch and talk to that old lawman. I'm a peaceable man, Susan, but I'm ready to go to war at this minute. I've never felt this kind of anger and hurt in my life and I believe I could kill Curly Joe Simpson should I happen into him."

"Oh, Nate, no. No, Nate," she sobbed. "I don't understand what brought all this on."

"Greed and a disdain for doing what's right." Coppersmith shoved his battered old hat down, slipped into a heavy blanket coat, and walked out. "Chapman better have some good reasons for this. I'll be home for supper and, in the morning, I'm riding to Doherty's." Susan was sobbing, holding her six-year-old daughter Ginny tight to her as she listened to him ride off to see the land agent.

Frail little Ginny, so small for her six years, was suscep-tible to every disease known to inhabit winter weather. Susan held the whimpering child in her arms and carried her to her bed. "Your papa will get this straightened out, I'm sure. That Mr. Simpson seemed so willing to help, to take care of the ranch while we get you well. There must be some kind of mistake."

"You're damn right I'm angry," Coppersmith said, standing in front of Reginald Chapman's heavy oak desk in an office building just half a block from the Humboldt County Court-house. "I want an answer and I mean right now."

"It's rather simple, Mr. Coppersmith," Chapman said. He was a thin man, had thinning hair and no facial hair, pale complexion, pale eyes, and was incapable of smiling. At five feet and six inches, he would have been looking at Copper-smith's belt if the two were standing together.

"The Homestead Act is precise in what is required and you didn't follow the rules. You abandoned your homestead, Mr. Coppersmith. Plain and simply, you have forfeited your claim to that land." He wore a smug look, all but saying "you're a fool."

He sat behind his massive oak desk drumming his fingers on the highly polished wood, reached for a cheroot and took more time than necessary getting it lit. Prissy is the first word that came to Coppersmith's mind and he knew he could pick the man up and simply fling him through the large windows that looked down on the well-kept courthouse property. *Smug little bastard was given lies by Curly Joe and I'm going to have to prove that. I see what has happened and I know I need help.*

"I abandoned nothing, Mr. Chapman. My daughter was very ill, it was the middle of winter, and I put my ranch foreman in charge until I could return, then brought my family to Winnemucca for the duration."

"That isn't what Joseph Simpson told me. He said you simply rode off and left the place. He never received any word from you in more than eight months and believed you had abandoned the property. By law, he filed to recover the claim."

"Liar!" Nate Coppersmith stormed. "I rode out there several times to give instructions for winter feeding, for spring birthing, for summer grazing. He lied, Chapman."

"If you have any proof of that, bring it to my attention, Mr. Coppersmith." The prim and proper little man sat back in his chair, gave his fingernails a good looking over which indicated the conversation was ended. "Until then, that homestead belongs to Mr. Simpson. Now, if you'll excuse me, I have other business to attend to."

"Proof?" Coppersmith stormed again. "What kind of proof?"

"Did you write out your instructions to Mr. Simpson? Give him directions in writing? You say you visited him. He says you rode off and he's not seen you since."

"Bah! You've not heard the last from me, Chapman. That's my homestead and you know damn well Curly Joe Simpson is stealing it." Chapman simply waved him off and Coppersmith fled the office, growling like a mad dog in his rage. The thought didn't enter his mind until he was almost home. What did Curly Joe Simpson offer this puny little land agent? Are the two of them in this together? Get me off the place, sell off the market steers, and then sell the place? I've got to see Seamus Doherty as soon as I can get up there.

It was just eighteen months ago that Simpson had ridden onto Coppersmith's ranch, not long after the battles the army had with the Bannock tribes in the area. Coppersmith's place had been hit twice by rampaging Indians; he'd lost buckaroos and cattle but the buildings and his family survived.

Little Ginny caught some kind of illness that fall, a major winter was developing and Susan wanted Nate to bring the family to Winnemucca for the winter. Simpson made him aware that with his extensive background in ranching that he could keep the ranch safe and Nate took the bait like a hungry carp.

"I've never been this humiliated in my life, Susan," he said when he got home from the meeting with the land agent. He had come straight back to their little rented cabin despite the fact he wanted to stop again at the stockyards. "To think I was helping my family and what I did was give away everything we've worked for. Maybe I should talk with Sheriff Peters before I ride up to Doherty's place."

"Don't forget he blames you for him being all stove up, Nate. You might not get much help from him."

"I told him not to get off his horse to tend that calf until I put a loop on the big mama cow. He was always so arrogant, so willing to not listen to anyone. Oh, no, don't listen to the boss-man, and sure enough that heifer whupped on him bad, tore up my horse while I tried to get to him. Damn fool."

"Maybe today isn't the right time to talk to Ephraim, Nate. Let's have a nice supper with the children and you can ride north to Paradise Valley tomorrow and spend some time with Mr. Doherty. He's a wise old man, Nate, and he's been a good friend for a long time."

"You're right, Susan. I'd probably shoot old Ephraim Peters the first time he mocked me. He never was a very good cowman and he's not much as a sheriff, either." They had to chuckle at his comment and Susan called the children for supper. Their oldest son Sam was eight years old and would be a big man like his father and baby Ralph, now four, never slowed down, whether moving, talking, or eating.

Sam was wise for his young age, had heard much of what Nate and Susan talked about. "I'll help you get our ranch back, Papa. I can help."

"I know you can, son. I might just need your help, too." He ruffled the boy's thick hair and chucked him gently under the chin. I must have been a mighty soft touch to Curly Joe Simpson and those friends of his. But someone a lot smarter than Simpson has to be behind all this.

CHAPTER TWO

"This is going to be a fine time, Seamus. How long has it been that we've had a bottle of the old home sitting between us?" Terrence Corcoran had left his badge on his desk in Eureka, Nevada the week before, taking some time off from chasing bad guys and making a long trek northward to the Paradise Valley of Humboldt County after getting a letter from an old family friend.

"Don't be putting the old blarney to your talk, Corcoran," Seamus Doherty said with a gentle laugh. "You've never put a foot in Ireland, have no natural brogue, and wouldn't know a real Irish spud if it spoke to you." He sat back in a heavy timbered chair covered in cowhide that had been laced into place and laughed right out loud.

Doherty had quit his job with Wells Fargo as a railroad detective for the life he had now. He'd been on this big cattle ranch in the Paradise Valley of northern Humboldt County for many years. The Doherty family had emigrated with the Corcoran clan on the same ship but Seamus Doherty was ten years old at the time and Corcoran hadn't been born until the ship was at sea for several days.

"Your letter said the antelope are fat and sassy and the mule deer are beggin' to be shot, and I'm here because of that," Corcoran said. He lifted his glass of fine Kentucky bourbon, approved of its color and aroma, and took it down in one swallow. "That's a fine mellow taste, that is. I rode through a range full of Herefords, Seamus. All of those yours?"

"Many have my brand, Terrence. This is fine cattle country. You need to give up this life of yours, carrying a badge and chasing outlaws, buy a fine spread, find a lovely lass, and settle down. Of course, she'd have to be blind if she picked you," he chuckled. "Then you two could have twelve kids, a thousand head of cattle, and a quiet life."

Humboldt County was large even by western standards and the Paradise Valley was about forty miles or so north of the county seat, Winnemucca. Its western edge was the lofty Santa Rosa Mountains from which cold streams and creeks, teeming with trout, watered the valley. Ranches great and small dotted the area, a small community existed, and the ranches raised cattle, sheep, grasses, and grains.

"Ha!" Corcoran laughed right out at the comment. "I wouldn't last a week, old man. Now, the finding of a lovely lass, I'll go along with. Marrying her and raising twelve children I won't abide. Don't tell anyone, Seamus, but I don't even know how to throw a lariat." He laughed right out again and whopped Doherty across the shoulders.

"No, old man, I'll carry my little tin star, put fear in the hearts of bad men, and chase after a wench or two should I run into them. After all, Seamus, isn't that what you did for so many years?"

Seamus Doherty smiled and nodded, remembering all those years traveling from Dodge City to San Francisco or south to Santa Fe, protecting trainload after trainload of gold, bank notes, and personal property. And catching bad men as often as possible. He also remembered how good it felt to hang up the gunbelt and take off the badge.

The two men were sitting in the large great room at Seamus Doherty's ranch, a blazing fire chasing off an early winter or late fall storm, waiting for Mrs. Doherty, Meagan by name, to call them for supper. The fireplace was built with native river rock, the house built with native timber that Doherty had cut and notched himself. There were steer horns mounted over the fireplace, a buffalo head and a couple of antelope heads mounted on the walls, and a great bear skin slung over the back of the leather-covered sofa Corcoran was sitting on.

"It feels comfortable, Seamus, I have to say that, but it just wouldn't work for me. I need to ramble about. You know, this job in Eureka is the longest I've ever worked for one man in my life. Must be gettin' old." He laughed.

Corcoran was long and strong, had reddish-gold hair that hung in waves and curls, a massive walrus moustache that he took great care of, and sparkling bright green eyes that drove the women mad. Corcoran could be serious when it mattered but more often than not he would be found with a grand smile, a wry smile, or just a crooked grin, probably thinking of some way to get in trouble. He was in his late thirties but acted more like a young buck out on a toot, chasing the elephant.

Those close to the lawman knew he enjoyed a party almost as much as he enjoyed a good knock 'em down fist fight. He could draw his Colt with lightning speed but told anyone willing to listen that hitting the target is more important than a fast draw.

"Heard the Bannock's were raising lots of dust up this way, Seamus. Still a problem?"

"Army boys at Fort McDermitt got 'em quieted down some, got some help from the local tribes and that helped.

Most of the trouble was northwest of us, up along the Oregon border, and down into the Black Rock Desert. Bannock's got some help from the Pitt River tribe and from the Western Shoshone. It was fierce for a while but things are back to normal now."

Corcoran snorted a bit at that wondering if there was such a thing as normal. "Normal, eh," he said. "That's a far-fetched idea, Seamus. But I think I know what it is you're trying to say. Would Indian trouble, cattle rustling, stage-coach robberies, along with murder and mayhem be consid-ered normal?" They had to laugh at the thought.

Meagan Doherty walked into the great room and the men jumped to their feet. She was tall, statuesque, and gorgeous. "I think it's time to put away the tall tales, boys, and join me for some supper." Her long red hair hung in great waves, her eyes so green they blazed, and her smile lit the northern skies was the way Seamus described his lovely wife.

"Seamus cut some steaks from a beef's ribs yesterday, Terrence. You might not need that knife you carry," she joked, leading them into a grand kitchen. It was at least forty feet in every direction with a massive cast iron cook stove, large carving and preparing counters, and a heavy oak table in the center of the room. There was room for at least eight people at the table, maybe ten if crowded just a bit.

Seamus took an end seat with Meagan to his left and Terrence to his right. "Usually we'll have some of the crew with us for supper," Seamus said. "The gang of them are off bringing the last of the strays down from summer range. We'll take the bunch of them to the feedlot next week."

Supper was filled with talk of the old days when Terrence was a boy and Seamus was ready to head west. Talk about Meagan arriving in San Francisco and meeting this huge monster of a Wells Fargo detective after having her possessions stolen. The lamps burned late, and didn't come back on too early the next morning.

"We'll pack the mules after a good breakfast, Terrence. I think I'll need more than just coffee to get my head out of the fog that's rolled in."

Meagan had platters of bacon and griddlecakes with fresh churned butter and molasses on the table and a pot of coffee boiling on the stove. "Hope old man winter holds off for a week, Seamus. I'm looking forward to just living out of a deer camp and riding through these beautiful mountains you have here."

Paradise Valley sat at the eastern base of the Santa Rosa Mountains about forty miles or so north of Winnemucca. Rocky and cut with deep canyons, covered with a hefty blanket of snow in the winter that fed rich ranch land in the valley, the mountains teemed with big game and game birds. Grasses in the valley were deep and lush allowing for ample grazing or cutting for winter feed.

"We'll need it to be a bit on the cold side, Terrence. Gets the buck deer and bull elk excited about finding the girls, you know. Makes them a little easier to find." He laughed. "Last fall, Meagan shot three deer and two antelope for some fine winter meat, and I managed to down two quail. Don't challenge that woman, Terrence. She could have outshot Doc Holliday any day of the week."

"Well maybe Holliday; he couldn't hit the broad side of a fat mule. But could she outshoot Bill Cody?" All Seamus Doherty did was smile and nod getting a giggle from Meagan.

"Let's move boys," Meagan said. "Don't get started on your stories until we're in a good camp high on a rocky ridge." She stopped talking suddenly and cocked her head to listen. "Sounds like someone coming up the road, Seamus."

The three of them walked to the front door to see who would be calling this early in the morning. "Why, my goodness and all that," Meagan Doherty said. "It's Nate Coppersmith." She waved and the three stepped off the veranda-style front porch to welcome their visitor.

CHAPTER THREE

"This is one of the sweetest deals you've ever come up with, Curly, but how long is it going to last?" Slant Eyed Tom sat on the porch of the Sleepy U ranch north of the Pueblo Valley. Until just three weeks ago the ranch had been owned by Nathaniel Coppersmith and his wife Susan.

The same argument had taken place several times over the last several days with Curly Joe Simpson getter more and more angry. Simpson was the type of man who wouldn't tolerate another challenging his position of leadership. In this case, leadership over a three-man gang of ruthless murderers, cutthroats, and thieves. To question Simpson was a sign of disrespect that simply wouldn't be tolerated.

Slant Eyed Tom was there the night Simpson shot his favorite dove in that little border town for asking why he never changed his shirt. Rockefeller laughed and said it was so dirty he couldn't take it off, which made the girl laugh for the last time in her life.

Interestingly, ever since that episode, Curly Joe Simpson has never been seen in anything but clean, rather fancy, clothing.

"I'm just saying your plan worked perfectly, Curly Joe. How much longer can this last?"

"How many times are you going to ask that? It'll last as long as we will," he stormed. His eyes narrowed down, his jaw tightened, and he glared at Slant Eye. "We're in, Slant Eye. Won't never have to run from a posse ever again. Won't never have to eat cold bacon and hard beans, or drink cold water for breakfast. No, sir, never again."

Simpson was going against the original plan but Slant Eye didn't know what the original was. The plan was to take over that ranch and sell it quick. Simpson, the proud and fancy now, wanted to play the part of Grandee, Lord of the Manor, Cattle Rancher.

Slant Eyed Tom O'Neil could see the flaw in Curly Joe's plans even if no one else in the so-called gang could. Lawmen all over the west would have posters with their pictures soon and they needed to finish this fine job they started. They managed to steal an entire ranch and fine herd of cattle. Finish the job, Slant Eye kept preaching to deaf ears. Sell this place before someone finds out who we are was his plea.

"How much do you know about being a cowman, Curly Joe? I don't know nothin'. You may have flummoxed old Coppersmith, outfoxed that fool land agent, but what we gots to do now is sell this place and get the hell out of this territory." Visions of a sheriff riding in with a posse, federal marshals brandishing warrants, or even a wild bunch of Coppersmith's friends riding up to the ranch had flooded his mind for days.

Curly Joe Simpson actually had worked as a ranch hand once, he could truthfully tell someone, but the work was mostly mucking out barn stalls and sloppin' hogs. He could talk the talk but sure as shootin' couldn't walk the walk. He talked good enough to get hired by Nate Coppersmith as ranch foreman. Coppersmith's ranch was a hundred miles from anywhere and keeping good hands was impossible. The fact that Simpson actually wanted to work for him should have sent signals of a problem in the making.

"I ain't plannin' on sellin' out, Slant Eye. I'm gonna live the life of a big time cattle rancher. Raise some prime beef, eat like a European king or something, and have me a beautiful young wife. That's what I'm gonna do." He strutted around the kitchen table, his chin jutting out some, and looked like a character out of some theater troupe.

"You're not thinking, Curly Joe. This was a good plan and it worked. You can't run this place, I know I can't, sure as hell dumbass Rockefeller can't. Sure as all get out somebody will come up with paper on one of us. No, we gots to stay on our plan."

"I don't much care for you talking to me that way, Slant Eyed Tom." Curly Joe Simpson's eyes narrowed down some, his jaw tightened, and his hand slowly made its way to the handle of a big forty-five revolver hanging at his side. "This was my plan all along, Slant Eye. My plan. This is my ranch now. Mine. You and Rocky work for me. I'm the boss and you'll do as I say." He was livid, gone from the amiable young man having morning coffee with a ranch hand to a psychotic killer.

His madness had been proven many times, most recently at a bank job in New Mexico when he lined up the cashiers and forced the bank manager to shoot each one, laughing wildly when the manager failed to hit the first man. He jerked the weapon from the old man, shot him six times, reloaded, and shot the cashiers point blank.

Simpson's body was tensed like a tiger at the attack and Slant Eyed Tom O'Neil slowly set the coffee pot back on the stove and turned to face the outlaw. "You got to get your head back on straight, Curly Joe." Slant Eye had never given thought about going up against his long-time friend. He knew Simpson was fast, a good shot, but knew that he was, too.

Curly Joe was standing at the table, a coffee mug in his left hand, his right hovering close to that big hog leg hanging near his waist. He turned away from Slant Eyed Tom, almost dismissing the man.

The two of them had no trouble taking that bank in Austin, Nevada. Rode up from Arizona Territory after taking three banks down that way and had burned more money in the last year than they ever thought even existed. Hell, Slant Eye thought, he had killed four men, Rocky Rockefeller two, and Curly Joe had wiped out three men who had been chasing them.

"Joe, there's paper all over this country, or soon will be, with our names and pictures on them. We gotta sell this place and get out of here."

"Why don't you just get on your horse and ride on out of here, then," Simpson said. "Don't need no more sniveling from you."

"Maybe I will, Curly Joe. Maybe it's time we settled up and I just rode off."

"Settle up? What's that supposed to mean? We ain't got no settling up to do."

"We do indeed have some settling up to do. I want my third. I want what's coming to me."

Simpson spun around, big heavy Colt in hand, and shot Slant Eyed Tom O'Neil. Slant Eye never got his hand close to the handle of his weapon, was flung back several feet, and slumped to the floor, eyes fastened on the ceiling of the ranch house kitchen, a big hole in the middle of his chest. "All settled up, Slant Eye," Simpson said, ejecting the empty shell from his pistol and putting in a fresh cartridge. He was standing at the stove pouring coffee when Rocky Rockefeller came hustling in.

"What's the shooting?" He stopped quickly when he spotted Slant Eyed Tom on the floor, bleeding heavily, moaning softly. "What's going on, Curly Joe?"

"Just you and me now, Rocky. Go to the barn and find that fool Indian. We all need to sit down for a long discussion on how the ranch is going to be operated." Simpson didn't give a second thought to O'Neil, slowly bleeding out just a few feet away. "We'll bury Slant Eyed Tom when he dies."

The fool Indian in the barn was Dancing Antelope, a Northern Paiute who lived with a Shoshone tribe near the Oregon border. He had worked part time for Coppersmith and had stayed on with Curly Joe Simpson.

The tribe was building a small community of mixed whites and Indians with help from the army stationed at Fort McDermott, many miles to the east. Their little community was just a few miles south of Grant County in Oregon.

Coppersmith spent some time telling Dancing Antelope why he was going to be living in Winnemucca for a while and Dancing Antelope didn't fully realize exactly what Simpson had done. All he knew was, Coppersmith was his friend. Nate Coppersmith asked him one time how old he was.

"Don't know," Dancing Antelope said. "Maybe thirty, maybe more. No need to count years once a man knows why there is a difference between men and women."

Coppersmith almost fell to the ground laughing at that answer. The two were good friends, hunted and fished together, worked hard on the ranch, and understood the differences in their backgrounds.

"What you want, Curly Joe?"

"You've been working this ranch for a couple of years,

Dancing Antelope. I want you to teach Rocky here how to move the cows from one range to another. He needs to learn that."

Rockefeller stiffened at Simpson's words and Dancing Antelope could see the man's jaws tighten up some. "What's the matter, Rocky-man, you don't know how to work cattle? Sure, by golly, I'll learn you how. Gonna be snow time soon, Rocky-feller, so we need to bring cattle to winter feeding grounds."

"Don't call me that, injun." Rockefeller hated Indians in the first place, had never worked on any kind of ranch since running away from his family's worthless dirt farm in Mississippi thirty years ago. "My name's Rockefeller."

"Sure, by golly, it is. Rocky-man and Rocky-feller same thing, eh? OK, Rocky-feller, let's go saddle up." Dancing Antelope had just the slightest grin on his craggy old face as he headed for the kitchen door.

"I ain't gonna work with no injun, Curly Joe."

"You will if I say so, Rocky. Take Slant Eyed Tom's body out and bury it and then saddle up to learn how to work with them cows of mine."

"Yours? Don't you mean ours?" Just the slightest hint of dawn crept into Rockefeller's slow brain system. "This is all ours, ain't it, Curly Joe?"

"Yes, of course it is. Now do as you're told." It was like he was talking to a ten-year-old but there was no gentle pat on the head, just an ugly sneer.

"Nate Coppersmith, I want you to meet one of my dearest friends. Shake hands with Terrence Corcoran. What brings you out here this time of the morning and in such a rush? Is there a problem?"

"How do you do, Mr. Corcoran. Oh, Seamus, they've

stolen my ranch, they're selling my cattle. What am I going to do?" Coppersmith was shaking in his fury and fear, was speaking so fast Terrence almost couldn't understand him.

Terrence Corcoran took this time to size up this visibly upset visitor and saw a big man with immense strength, but fear and anger in his eyes. He had a rifle tucked on his saddle and carried a heavy side arm. This was a worried cattleman, Terrence thought, who would be one hell of an adversary in a fight. But his weapons were for range work; he's no kind of gunman at all though he'd sure hate to go up against him without a gun.

"Calm down, Nate. Tie off your horse, get a handle on whatever it is, and let's find a comfortable chair and a hot cup of coffee. Then, nice and slow, tell me whatever this dreadful thing is." Seamus Doherty was a sea of calm to Nate's furious tempest and he had to take the lead rope from the man and tie off his horse for him. He took him by the elbow and led him up onto the porch and into the great room to sit by the fire.

"Meagan darling, would you bring us a pot of coffee and then join us? Mr. Coppersmith has a problem that we need to hear about." With nods and hand gestures, Doherty managed to get the three men settled into massive chairs before a roaring fire. "That's better," he said. "Now, Nate, nice and slow, tell us what has happened."

Meagan brought a large pot of coffee and hung it on a swinging hook by the fire, then went back for a tray which was filled with mugs and a platter of sweet cinnamon rolls. "Yes, Nate," she said. "You look like the wrath, if you'll pardon me saying so. How is little Ginny?"

"Thank you, Meagan; I feel like the wrath. My daughter's much better. In fact, we were contemplating returning to the ranch within the next week or so." His face changed from friendly to seething anger as he finished that comment. "Oh, Seamus, they've stolen my ranch."

"Now, Nate, please. Calm yourself and tell us what this is all about." Seamus took a cinnamon roll and settled back in his big chair. "If something's been stolen, remember, old friend, you're amongst some fine old law-dogs here." He chuckled. "Terrence Corcoran still carries a badge despite himself." Coppersmith gave Terrence a quick glance at that statement.

"When Ginny got so sick, Susan needed to have her close to medical help and I had hired a man, Joe Simpson, to be my ranch foreman. I told him I had to take my family to Winnemucca so Ginny would be near medical help and told him to run the ranch until I got back. We planned on being in town for at least a year, Seamus."

"I see nothing wrong with that, Nate. Go on," Doherty said. Terrence Corcoran straightened up a little in his chair and cocked his head just a bit.

"Yes, Mr. Coppersmith, go on. I think I can see what it is you are about to tell us. Did this Simpson feller have a nickname? For instance, Curly Joe Simpson? And did he bring his own buckaroos with him? Would one of them be named Tom O'Neil?"

"You seem to know a lot about this, Terrence," Doherty said. "Go on, Nate, I'm most interested."

Nathaniel Coppersmith gave Corcoran more than a hard stare. "Yes, Mr. Corcoran, to both your questions." He wiped sweat from his forehead, drank a swill of coffee and continued. "Simpson has gone to the federal land agent, that filthy Reginald Chapman, claiming I have abandoned the ranch and property and, therefore, my homestead is vacant and Simpson has in turn filed on it. Chapman says everything is legal because I can't prove in writing what I claimed. That

Simpson was hired to run my ranch while I took care of my sick daughter."

"That's horrible," Meagan Doherty said. "Have you gone to the sheriff? What did Peters say about all that?"

"He still blames me for his injuries and won't even talk to me. He's threatened to sue me, and wouldn't help me if it meant his own life. No, I can't go to the Humboldt County Sheriff on this." His eyes filled with tears, his shoulders shaking as he tried to hold back his sobs.

"That ranch is all Susan and I ever wanted. We've ridden every square inch of those one hundred sixty acres, Seamus. I have grazing rights on three sections of land that I share with other ranchers in the area; there are only four of us out there, along with a tribe of Shoshone Indians that are setting up a permanent place to live. The army's helping them.

"There's good water, good grass for that area, and my small herd has been growing every year I've been there. It's a five-year homestead, Seamus, and we've been there three years now. My home, barns, and herd have been stolen and nobody will help."

He finally broke down, the sobs wracking his large body and Meagan Doherty moved over to console the man. "I think there just might be somebody here who can help, Mr. Coppersmith." Terrence Corcoran picked a cinnamon roll from the platter and poured himself another cup of coffee.

"Wouldn't have a wee bit of brandy for this, would you, Seamus?" Corcoran's eyes had a glint to them and a bit of a smile creased his face as he let Seamus Doherty pour some fine brandy in his coffee mug. If there was one thing in the world that would make Terrence Corcoran turn from amiable to vicious, it was someone taking advantage of someone who couldn't fight back.

Corcoran was the underdog's best friend and nothing riled

him more than what he had just heard from Coppersmith. "What exactly did the land agent tell you?"

"He almost called me a liar when I said I had visited Simpson at least twice to make sure things were being run right. He asked if I had proof that I visited. Asked if I had given written instructions to Simpson. Even if I had, Simpson would have them, not me. I wonder if Chapman isn't involved in some way?"

So did Corcoran. It wouldn't be the first time a federal agent was involved in land fraud, and this was purely and simply land fraud. If Chapman and Simpson were working in cahoots, then that ranch and everything on it would come up for sale in the very near future. Coppersmith had said his herd was already at the feedlot so one would think only the cows, fresh heifers, and bulls would be at the ranch. A perfect time to sell it.

"Would you give me a bit of time, Mr. Coppersmith, to work on this problem of yours? Tell me about your ranch, any employees you might have there besides this Simpson feller and his crew, and the layout of the place. I haven't worked as a buckaroo for a few years but I'll bet I can get a job at your ranch and, if I can, you'll have it back, pronto."

"See, Coppersmith? No need to get yourself all riled up." Seamus smiled, grabbing another cinnamon roll. "Not when Terrence Corcoran is available to get involved. Why, I remember once...," and he took a gentle poke in the ribs from Meagan. "Well, maybe that can wait just a bit, eh?"

Corcoran and Coppersmith walked out onto the large veranda porch and down the steps to the barnyard and corrals. They wandered about the Doherty ranch for the next couple of hours before coming back into the large kitchen and warm cook stove. Coppersmith was far more settled this time, even wearing the briefest of a smile.

"If I can borrow a pack mule and some gear, Seamus, I'll light out right away for Coppersmith's place and find that Indian he told me about. Looks like we'll not be hunting mule deer and antelope, my friend, but I will be doing some hunting." The long talk with Nate as they wandered through Doherty's place had given Corcoran plenty of time to come with an idea to get that ranch back.

"I think I see your plan, Terrence, but I have to remind you that this Curly Joe Simpson sounds very much like a psychopathic killer to me. You said you saw posters before you left Eureka? That means that Sheriff Peters should also have them. While you're up north, I might just ride into town and talk with that man."

"That's something I'm going to leave in your hands, Seamus. This Sheriff Pete Peters sounds like an angry old man to me, not a law-dog. If Simpson and Chapman are working together, don't be surprised if Peters is in on it. That property and herd is worth considerable money, and I'll get Simpson out of the picture before he can sell it.

"You see what you can find out from Peters and Chapman but do your best to keep Coppersmith away from the two of them. He's not a gunman, Seamus. He'll just get himself killed."

CHAPTER FOUR

"It's okay, Rube, it's only about a hundred miles or so 'till the next warm stall for you," he said to his long time friend, Rube the horse. "You should have known when we left Eureka that this wouldn't just be a little hunting trip I'd be taking." Long journeys through Nevada's great open valleys spread out between high north-south mountain ranges were designed for long conversations with one's horse or other suitable companion.

"I think we'll find a new friend in this feller Coppersmith called Dancing Antelope. Always have liked the Paiute people. They have the best sense of humor of any people I know, exceptin' of course, us Irishers." He wasn't trying to make good time moving northwest from the foot of the Santa Rosa Mountains and spent the first night under a cottonwood tree alongside a muddy waterhole.

Morning found him following what some called the Queen's River and others called Quinn's River. "This should take us close enough that we can scout out Coppersmith's place sometime tomorrow, Mr. Rube, and it looks like we might just have a storm bearing down on us. We should have expected that, eh old man?"

Riding was fast and relatively easy alongside the mostly dried up streambed but late in the afternoon, the winds kicked up from the north, black clouds boiled across the open sky, and when it was about time to make camp, icy rain pelted Terrence Corcoran, Rube, and the pack mule. "Those trees over there have our names writ large, Rube. Time to make camp."

Dancing Antelope and Rocky Rockefeller rode into the main ranch about mid-day and took their horses to the corrals. Rocky didn't say a word, didn't wipe down his horse, just jerked the rig off and turned the gelding into the corral. Dancing Antelope snickered some, shaking his dark head. He caught up with the animal and took care of it along with his own. "Foolish man, this Rocky-feller. Foolish man."

"I ain't workin' with that injun no more, Curly Joe. No more," he snarled, pulling himself out of his winter coat and walking to the cook stove. He poured half a cup of coffee. "Where's the whiskey?"

"You get them cows moved like I told you?" Simpson was dressed in a white shirt, pale blue, almost gray, wool vest, and wool pants. He was wearing a pair of fancy gambler style high-heeled boots, and silver mounted spurs. Dressed as a large and successful rancher might be at the hotel after a big fall sale of his market-ready steers.

Curly Joe Simpson hadn't done a lick of work around the ranch since he shot Slant Eyed Tom three days ago but dressed in the finest clothing that old Nate Coppersmith had in his closet, even if some of it didn't exactly fit proper like.

"Answer me, Rocky. Did you move them cows?"

"They're moved and if you want more of 'em moved,

you're movin' 'em. That injun thinks he can tell me what to do and when to do it, he's gonna find out what my Colt was made for. And my knife." He was still looking around the kitchen for the jug and asked again, "Where's the whiskey?"

"It's in the cabinet, fool. Until I can replace Slant Eye, you'll work with Dancing Antelope. He knows about cows and this ranch and you'll do as I say. Pour me a cup of that stuff, too."

"Get your own damn whiskey," Rocky said, pouring his cup full and putting the bottle back in the cabinet. He stood next to the hot cook stove glaring at Curly Joe.

Simpson all at once realized that he was in a bad situation and he better make it a good situation fast. Despite his quick temper and his anger, he all but ambled to the cabinet and pulled the bottle out. "Don't get yourself all riled up, Rocky. We got us a sweet deal here and we got to make it work. You learn what you can from the Indian and we won't need him anymore.

"We find a couple of dumb old punchers and you'll be my ranch foreman with them working for you. It shouldn't take a smart feller like you just a few days to learn this cow business from that Indian. Here, let me pour you another drink, Mr. Foreman."

"I thought what we talked about when you brought me an' Slant Eye up here was the plan, Curly Joe? We're not gonna sell the ranch and move on? I don't like that injun, don't like them cows, and don't want to be here."

"We changed the plans because we can make a lot more money by keeping this ranch. You won't be working with Dancing Antelope for long and you'll have your own crew working the cows. You won't have to do nothing, Mr. Foreman."

James "Rocky" Rockefeller stood a little taller, let his shoulders set a bit stiffer, and offered his mug to Simpson. "I kinda like the sound of that, Curly Joe. I didn't know that was your plan."

"Tomorrow, you just go right out there with Dancing Antelope and learn about this cow business. And talk to the man, find out if there are any men available to work on the ranch. We get rid of the Indian, you're gonna need a couple of hands to work with you."

Rocky Rockefeller was a fired up buckaroo the next morning heading through six inches or so of fresh snow toward the barn to meet up with Dancing Antelope. "I better not tell that dumb injun that I'm gonna be the new foreman around here but he better not give me no trouble or I will shoot him dead. Ain't never scalped me an injun before, but I surely will scalp this one." He laughed the whole time saddling up.

"We got about a hunnert pregnant heifers we gotta move down out of them rocks, Rocky-feller, so let's get movin'," Dancing Antelope said. "You make your circle from the north and I'll start mine from the southwest, and we'll move them into the grass alongside that stream. They can spend the winter near the pond.

"Gotta keep 'em movin' though. Don't give 'em a chance to drift off on you. Might be a little slick up there, too, but we gotta get 'em down in case this storm really boils in. Let's ride," he said, heading off to the southwest to start his big circle.

A good buckaroo can move many head of cattle by himself as he makes a gather and a small herd will usually be led by one dominant animal, the others trailing along. Keeping 'em going downhill isn't difficult but breaking them out from where they're comfortable, warm, and feeding takes learning. Rocky Rockefeller wasn't in a learning mood.

"Yeah, injun, let's ride," Rockefeller muttered under his breath, glaring at the big Paiute. He mounted up and set off at a trot through heavy snow to begin a long day of moving cows out of a rocky mountainside where they felt safe from cowboys interfering in their lives. Great stands of pine, fir, and cedar dotted the hillsides, and deep canyons split them often. There were bluffs and swales, gentle slopes, and incredibly steep banks that offered the cattle hiding places and escape routes. Dancing Antelope had been working cattle for ten years, Rockefeller two weeks.

It was well after mid-day that Corcoran rode toward a saddle in the hillside he was following. 'If I'm still halfway good at figuring out where I am, I might see a ranch when I top that ridge," he declared. "I've never really been lost, you know that, don't you, Rube? I can tell you I'm here," and he pointed down at the ground, "but there have been times when I didn't exactly know where here was," and he chuckled some at his little joke.

He topped the ridge and off in the distance could see fenced-off fields and a complex of buildings that he figured was Coppersmith's place. "Looks to be nicely put together. Let's stay out of sight, Rube, and see what we can see." He rode down the side of the hill toward a pond. Off to the west was a rise of mountains and it looked like he could see some cattle drifting down toward the fields that surrounded the pond.

The snowstorm from the night before had let up considerably with great patches of blue sky that offered the chance of a bitter cold night coming up and fair weather tomorrow. Corcoran spotted a large stand of cottonwood and aspen half a mile from the pond and rode toward it.

"Good spot to set up camp and I should be able to keep an eye on the ranch from there."

As he neared the trees, up a slightly steep slope from the

pond, he saw the first of the herd drifting in and heard the singsong of a buckaroo urging them on. It was at least a half hour before the whole herd was pushed onto that open range of snow-covered grass, probably fifty or more cows and one lonely buckaroo.

"The man keeps lookin' around, like maybe he saw me, or he's waiting for someone else to come along." He had his camp set deep in the woods and felt the rider probably didn't see him. "They're inside the ranch boundaries, plenty of grass and water, so there won't be a night rider. No fire until that feller heads to the ranch."

Corcoran always carried a telescope he garnered from an army scout years ago and pulled it from the pack to take a good look at the man who was waiting for something or someone.

"Well now," he said quietly, holding the scope still. "If that ain't an Indian, I'll go without my coffee for a week. Haven't been here half an hour and I've found Dancing Antelope. He's a good cowman, too, from what I just watched." Corcoran sat with his back against the packsaddle and watched as Dancing Antelope got the herd settled along the banks of the pond, continually searching the hillsides to his north.

"Something's got that buzzard in a bit of a rile. Maybe there's another buckaroo out there with more cows. Sure looks like he's expecting someone or something. He's a big boy but I can see in those lines around his eyes that he's not an angry one. Man likes to laugh." Dancing Antelope circled the pond, at least ten acres in size, looking up into the hills to his north at every opportunity.

It was getting late in the afternoon and despite how much Corcoran wanted to keep watching, he had to get his camp set up or he'd be one frozen Irisher come morning. He built a nice fire ring with plenty of rocks to choose from and set his lean-to so he'd get full benefit from the fire. Gathering wood gave him a chance to look down at the pond often and he always found Dancing Antelope circling about, looking into the hills.

It was very close to dark when Corcoran spotted a line of cows slowly moving down out of the north hills toward the pond, and another half hour before most of the cows were down and a single buckaroo came into view. "That man might know how to ride a horse but he don't know much about moving cows. Betcha that's either Rockefeller or O'Neil."

Dancing Antelope spread the cows around the pond and the two riders headed off for the ranch complex about half a mile down slope. "I've got a good slab of smoked venison, a big pot for coffee, and a nip or two of brandy, and Mr. Dancing Antelope, you and I will meet tomorrow morning," Corcoran said, striking a flint to some black powder he had under a drift of kindling.

Corcoran felt the keen point of the knife at his throat and heard the soft voice of a man saying, "Don't move fast or you will ruin that blanket with your blood."

He was awake and alert immediately, didn't move and took half a second to contemplate what was said and how it was said. Paiute Indians speaking English have a distinctive lilt, almost musical, to their accent and Corcoran smiled, despite the keen knife-edge at his throat.

"Would you be Dancing Antelope?" he asked. He had to keep as calm as possible, knew his weapons were not within reach, and hoped he was right about who he thought held the deadly blade.

"Maybe," the man said. "I don't know you. Why would you know Dancing Antelope?"

"My name is Corcoran, Terrence Corcoran, and I'm here

to help Nate Coppersmith get his ranch back. He told me to find you to help. Looks like you found me."

The knife was slowly withdrawn and Corcoran scrambled out of his blankets to face a Paiute Indian at least his own size. He pulled his boots on, wrapped himself in a buffalo robe coat and got the fire stirred up and blazing, all the time sizing up this large man with a wicked knife. Dancing Antelope was walking around the camp, slowly, never taking his eyes off Corcoran, sizing up this large white man who asked for help.

Finally the two sat across from each other sharing the hot fire, waiting for the coffee to boil. "Are you aware, Dancing Antelope, of just how much trouble Nate Coppersmith is in? What is happening with him, Curly Joe Simpson, and this ranch?"

"I don't understand many of the ways of the white man, Terrence Corcoran, particularly this idea of owning something that was here before you were born and will still be here thousands of phases of the moon after you are dead. But to answer your question, yes, I know how much trouble my friend Nate is in.

"This Curly Joe man is an arrogant ass, Terrence, and he killed the man who actually knew something about a cattle ranch. The other man, this Rocky-Feller, is as stupid a man as I've met. He is the man that you saw come into the valley with the other heifers. He left many up in the rocks that I'll have to bring down before the heavy snows. So how is it you can help Nate? How is it I can help you?"

Corcoran felt an instant camaraderie with Dancing Antelope and could feel a depth, a level of tremendous wisdom in the man; he wondered if Nate Coppersmith was aware of what this Paiute could be capable of. He loved it when he got to work with people like this old Paiute. He's gonna learn a white man thing or two and Terrence was gonna learn a Paiute thing or two.

"You already have a good handle on the situation, Dancing Antelope. How much do you know about how Coppersmith came to own this property?"

"He called it homestead and he had to build home, and create working ranch within five years. He told me all about it. Don't know why Curly Joe thinks he owns place now."

Corcoran took the next half hour explaining how Curly Joe Simpson had coerced Coppersmith into believing that he would watch over the ranch while Nate watched over his family, then claimed that Nate abandoned the property.

"He didn't abandon," Dancing Antelope said immediately. "I was there, sitting at the table drinking coffee when he told Simpson to take care of the property while he took his family to Winnemucca for the winter."

Nate must have forgotten that Dancing Antelope heard what was said. Corcoran thought that might be Nate's answer to this, then the clouds of discouragement closed in. That wouldn't work because no court would accept the testimony of an Indian. One problem right after another.

"This Rocky-Feller asked me if I knew any white mens that could come to work on the ranch." Dancing Antelope had a wry grin splashed across his face and it was his eyes that were dancing. "Do you know anyone, Terrence Corcoran?" he asked.

"Indeed I do," the big man said. He too had a nice smile on his face as he poured coffee for the two.

"Before we go to the big ranch house, I think you should come to the village where I live and meet Betsy Shaggy Hair Schultz. She's a schoolteacher and she and Susan Coppersmith were good friends. She knows things, Terrence Corcoran."

If nothing else, Corcoran thought, the name alone would

guarantee that he would meet Shaggy Hair, the schoolteacher. He let his mind create multiple images of a woman known as Shaggy Hair.

"It will be my pleasure, old man." He tried for hours to create a picture in his mind of this creature called Betsy Shaggy Hair Schultz and with each passing frame, he chuckled or scowled or just waited for the next one. Shaggy Hair. I'm looking forward to meeting you, Miss Shaggy Hair, he thought.

CHAPTER FIVE

"Mornin' Pete. It's a cold one out there this morning." Seamus and Meagan had driven the buggy into town the previous day. Doherty had a team of pacers that he treated as family and gave them every opportunity to show their stuff. It was a long, full day's ride from Paradise Valley to Winnemucca but one filled with the beauty of the verdant valley surrounded by high mountain peaks.

Two prancing horses, trotters, pacers, a face full of cold autumn air, a lovely lady by his side, and Seamus felt twenty years younger on a ride like this one. "I'd best enjoy the ride," he muttered to Meagan. "It won't be nice bracing Sheriff Peters. If what Corcoran said about this Curly Joe Simpson and company is true, Peters should have arrested them on sight."

Seamus was going to get answers from the sheriff and Meagan was going to visit all the shops in the Humboldt County seat. Winnemucca was a thriving little town plunked down on the Humboldt River. The town was built along the water and the emigrant trail that brought so many from the east to the California gold fields. Winnemucca became a rail stop for the intercontinental railroad, and a crossroads for north/south travelers.

Meagan was well aware that the railroad brought fashions from San Francisco, New York, and Europe and she loved to look at them even if she knew she'd never wear any of them.

"Should I buy silk or satin dresses, Seamus? And would you care for a silk scarf or two?" She had to giggle saying it and then laugh when Seamus only gave out a grouchy little humph or two.

"I'll be seeing Peters and maybe that land agent, little darlin', so you just enjoy yourself," he said with a gleam in his eye that she knew would be coming.

"What brings the head honcho of Paradise Valley to the big city, Seamus? Lefty Tom Atkins said your cattle aren't in his sales yard yet."

"Boys'll have 'em down next week, Pete. What I want to talk to you about is what is happening with Nate Copper-smith and his ranch. You worked for him, you know he would never abandon that place."

"Yeah, I worked for him," Sheriff Ephraim 'Pete' Peters spat out. "That's why I'm all stove up. That man caused me to be the half cripple I am, Seamus. Don't look to me to help that bastard." Peters was, in his mind, a first class buckaroo before the mama cow and her calf accident, tall and rangy, tough in the muscle department and soft in the heart before the problems.

He was a changed man, not the least likeable, angry at the world, and blaming everyone and everything for his problems. In particular, he blamed Nathaniel Coppersmith. He sat behind his heavy oak desk, a cup of hot coffee in front of him, glowering at Doherty.

"I heard that this Joe Simpson is a bank robber and killer,

Pete. There are posters out on the man. This is a criminal conspiracy to steal the Coppersmith ranch. It shouldn't be a personal thing between you and Nate."

"If you're trying to tell me what my job is, Seamus, you can put that coffee cup down and waltz right on out of this office. The federal land agent says it's a deal, it's a deal. Ain't my jurisdiction anyway. It's federal." He thumped the desk with his fist and glared at the big former Wells Fargo detective.

"Curly Joe Simpson is a wanted man, Sheriff. That is your jurisdiction."

"Get the hell out of my office, Seamus Doherty. This isn't your call, it isn't your problem, and it's not in my jurisdiction. Get out." He slammed his fist down on the desk and gave the impression he might even pull that heavy revolver he carried.

Doherty's eyes narrowed, his jaw tightened visibly, and he hunched over the desk. "I'll get out, Sheriff Peters," Doherty said. His anger and temper were rising fast but he kept himself in control. "You sure as hell haven't heard the last of this. Nate Coppersmith deserves better from you and the people of Humboldt County do, too. You're becoming an angry old man, Pete. This county deserves better." Seamus Doherty slammed the door behind him and stormed down the muddy streets of Winnemucca.

He found Meagan and led her to the café at their hotel. "That man has no right to wear a badge and he's a lucky one that it was I that marched into his office and not Terrence Corcoran. For the sheriff of a county like this to ignore three known killers as they take a man's ranch and livelihood should be a hanging offense." He was as incensed as she had ever seen him.

They were having an early lunch at the Winnemucca Hotel near the banks of the Humboldt River. "I tell you, Meagan," Seamus continued, "Nate is in more trouble than I imagined. Peters has washed his hands of the entire affair and that measly land agent won't even say hello more or less talk to me. Nate's only hope right now is Terrence Corcoran."

"If the land agent were a woman, Corcoran could walk in the door, offer one of his very special smiles, and Nate Coppersmith would have his ranch back that fast. Oh, he does have a wicked smile, Seamus."

"Don't start now, woman."

Her answer was just a tinkle of a laugh which got another glare from Doherty.

"You're just a little tease, Meagan," he said. He couldn't hold the glare any longer and had to chuckle which brought another little tinkle of laughter from Meagan. They spent the next hour discussing the possibility that the sheriff, land agent, and outlaws were working together with the aim of selling the ranch and splitting the money.

"Corcoran's the right man to end this fraud," Doherty said. "I just hope he can do it quickly enough. To make a plan like this work, that ranch has to be sold just as soon as possible. I should have ridden with him."

"No, no, Seamus. You put that badge away a long time ago."

"Will this Corcoran be able to get our ranch back, Nate? I feel so awful making you leave the place to bring me and the children to town. Little Ginny was so sick and I didn't think she'd live through the winter out there. Will you forgive me?" She almost begged.

"Don't be foolish, Susan. My family will always come first. I liked this Corcoran fella. Big and strong and something in his eyes that told me I could trust him, not just to do as he said he would, but trust the man with my life."

"That's what we're doing, Nate."

"Yes, it is. I'm going down to the stockyards and talk to Lefty Tom Atkins. I'm going to see if I can get him to hold off selling those steers for a short time. Hopefully, this will be all over with in just a few days."

"Don't get in trouble, Nate. You know your temper and you know how upset you are. Walk away from trouble, please." In all their years together, she had only seen Nate lose his temper once. They were walking down the street in Dodge City, waiting for the train, when a man made rude comments and attempted to show himself to her.

Nate Coppersmith beat the man into the mud of that trailhead city until three men, one wearing a badge, were able to pull him off. The lawman said it would have been justified if he had shot him, but, she remembered, Nate said he would remember a beating.

He smiled, gave her a little hug and kiss on the forehead, slouched into a heavy blanket coat and headed out for the stockyards. It was a short ride to the west along the rail lines to the yards. I'll stay out of trouble as long as nobody tries to give me any more trouble, he thought and smiled riding along the tracks. Corcoran said this Joe Simpson was a known bank robber and killer. If that's so, why hasn't Peters tried to arrest him? Did they zero in on my ranch on purpose? Was this a plan? I would never have thought such a thing, but it was Simpson's idea for Susan and me to spend the winter in town so little Ginny could get well. Somehow he got it into my head that I should go with Susan and the children and I allowed myself to be led like a lamb. I've embarrassed myself. I've destroyed Susan's life and threatened my family's existence.

Nate couldn't get the word conspiracy out of his head. This Simpson, outlaw that he was, partnering up with the land agent and the sheriff. Maybe Peters is behind all of this. His way of getting back at me. Using an outlaw and the land agent to break me. He could feel the anger building as he rode through the dusty little town toward one of the largest and busiest stockyards in the silver state. He concentrated for the next several minutes on calming himself down, remembering Susan's words of caution.

As he rode through the livestock property he saw just empty pens stretched out and got the bad news as soon as he walked into the offices. "No, no, Lefty, it isn't your fault. It's your job to sell and ship the cattle, and I understand the land agent has those papers saying Simpson has the homestead now. He won't for long, I tell you. He won't."

Nate turned to walk out of the office when he thought to ask, "Has anyone come in to claim the money from the sale?"

"That feller Simpson collected it in cash. Mostly these boys simply have the funds transferred to their banks but he wanted cash, said he had bills to be paid."

Coppersmith was trying to hold in the anger as he rode away from the stockyards and decided a cold beer might calm him down some. He didn't ask if the sale was a good one, he already knew it was. He tied off his horse in front of the Star Saloon and Restaurant because they offered the best free lunch in the county. Where the idea of the free lunch originated didn't interest Coppersmith but the idea of having one did even though he and Susan had had their meal. Food could be a calming influence as well as a cold beer.

He stood at the long bar that ran along the east wall of the narrow saloon, tables scattered along the west wall. A table filled with cheeses, fruits, meats, and breads was set up and all a customer had to do was buy a drink to partake. "A cold frothy one, Sam, if you please and I'll take that table by the window."

"I'll bring it right over, Nate. Have some splendid roast elk on the table today and some of Maurice's specially smoked ham, cut so thin you could read the Winnemucca Sun through it."

He was laughing as Nate walked to the table, chuckling as well. Roast elk and smoked ham for the price of a glass of cold beer. He would still have preferred a chunk of roast pork from Susan's Dutch oven at his own table in his own kitchen at his own ranch.

The anger at the situation was almost more than he could handle and it quickly took a turn for the worse as Humboldt County Sheriff Ephraim Peters came through the bat-wing doors. It seemed to Nate that the limping lawman went out of his way to scowl at him as he walked to the bar.

The sheriff ordered a beer and turned to face Copper-smith. "If you think Seamus Doherty is gonna change my mind about you, Coppersmith, you're wrong. You walked away from your ranch and lost it. Don't be blaming me." The few men in the saloon quit their card games, quit their conversations, and wondered just how long the sheriff had to live, challenging the likes of Nate Coppersmith.

What has Seamus said or done? And he's suggesting that he seems to know my questions of a conspiracy? He must be involved, Nate thought.

Nate could feel the redness begin half way down his back, crawl up his neck and flush his face full of desperate anger. "Curly Joe Simpson is a wanted man and you are supposed to be a sheriff. Nothing more needs be said. If you'd done your job right as a buckaroo, you'd still be one. Seems you can't do your job right as a sheriff either." Nate was hoping that maybe an open taunt would cause Peters to respond and fully impli-cate himself. Or maybe he just wanted to see if the fool would lose his temper and attack him.

Oh, Sheriff, please do that. Just walk those few steps to my table and take a swing. But I can see it in his eyes right now. He's afraid of me and knows that little tin badge isn't going to help if he swings first.

This is what Corcoran had seen at Doherty's ranch. A gunman would have thought about the sheriff drawing on him, not taking a swing at him. The idea of Peters going for his gun never entered Coppersmith's mind. Peters, though, was a former buckaroo, not a lawman and not a gunman either. His initial thoughts were on a good old fight and knew he could not stand up to Coppersmith.

There was not a large crowd yet in the Spur but those that were there got very quiet. Those closest to either man backed away and old Sam the barman knew he couldn't even call the sheriff for help. The dynamite was in the blast hole and tamped well, the fuse was lit, burning at forty-five seconds to the foot. Would something happen to stop the explosion that was so close to hand?

Peters looked around and realized what a terrible situation he was in. On the one hand, he was ready to square off with this rancher who destroyed his career as a cowman but he was the sheriff. Retribution, vengeance, getting even, whatever it is you wanted to call it, Peters knew his position as sheriff would be lost if he made even the slightest move right now.

Peters looked around the long narrow saloon and saw many faces primed for the fight; he saw people in the back, where the gaming rooms were, looking out at him and knew he had to walk out of the bar. It galled him to the quick, bile rose to his throat, but he turned his back to Nate, drank down his beer in one gulp, turned slowly and walked out the door.

It was a long time before conversations began and it was equally long before Nate fully understood just how close that situation was. He drank a swallow of his beer and left his food, nodded to Sam, and walked out. He's involved in some way with Simpson and the land agent, Nate thought. Otherwise he would have put up a fight, he would have created a situation in which I would break the law, giving him an opportunity to shoot me.

Nate couldn't get it out of his head that Seamus Doherty must have said something to the sheriff to make him react the way he did. He remembered clearly Seamus telling him to stay away from the sheriff, away from the land agent, that Corcoran would solve the problem. "Well, Seamus, then if Corcoran's going to solve this, why are you getting involved?" He realized at once that he was talking to himself, reddened a bit, and stepped quickly down the street.

Corcoran and Dancing Antelope were riding across a wide, almost flat piece of high prairie just a few miles south of the Oregon-Nevada border. "Our new village is on the border, Terrence, and there's an army camp just two day's ride. This mix of tribes has had its problems but things are quiet now."

"Who are you taking me to meet, and why?" Corcoran asked. Dancing Antelope had mentioned a school teacher named Betsy 'Shaggy Hair' Schultz but didn't go into any detail.

"We have a schoolhouse and Shaggy Hair is the teacher, but was a very close friend of Susan Coppersmith. She angry at what is happening, say bad things about Curly Joe. You like her, Corcoran. For white woman, very pretty. Not like most with turned down mouths and angry eyes."

Corcoran chuckled thinking that Dancing Antelope must have met some white women who didn't understand Paiute humor. I can just almost imagine some of the things he might have said to make a woman angry. He's impudent to start with, has a quick mind, a reckless sense of humor. Oh, my, what he might have said or done. He continued to chuckle as they rode along. I wonder why we haven't crossed trails?

The village was scattered about with a few wooden buildings, some well built and strong, others just thrown together. There were brush-covered hogans, a teepee or two, and even a few large squad tents, probably from the army. There was a small army detachment set up on the edge of the village.

A few people stared at the two as they rode down the dusty street. They passed a store selling fresh food, farm implements, and 'mules for rent'. It was half tent, half boards, and crowded. There were Indians in buckskins, soldiers in uniform, and buckaroos in dusty chaps milling about tables filled with goods.

Dancing Antelope nodded to many and Corcoran took in the sights. Indians dressed in full native costume mixed with Indians dressed in white man's clothing walked the streets with white buckaroos and army boys in blue. Children and dogs ran everywhere in dusty confusion; there was guitar music and plaintive singing coming from at least one building. Some tents indicated they were saloons, others were pleasure palaces, and Corcoran laughed and pointed at one. They rode up and stopped their horses in front of a single level building with clapboard siding. The hand-painted sign simply said 'School'.

Dancing Antelope didn't bother to knock on the door, just barged right in with Corcoran trailing close behind. There were ten or twelve school desks spread about a large room with a potbelly stove in the center. A strong wooden desk sat along one wall facing the school desks, and there was a large wall set for chalk use. "Our school," Dancing Antelope proclaimed.

He walked up to a doorway and knocked, standing back to wait for a response which came quickly. "Be right there. Just take your seat and open your books." Dancing Antelope chuckled and plunked himself down at the teacher's desk. Betsy 'Shaggy Hair' Schultz walked into the schoolroom and Corcoran's heart took a double pump.

She was tall, almost six feet, he thought, slim to being very thin but shapely as a woman should be. Her eyes were sky blue, her browned cheeks held a soft blush, and her lips were filled with a smile. It was the hair that held his gaze the longest. A squirrel's nest if he ever saw one. No, maybe more a pack rat's home. Her hair was so blonde it was almost white and it was filled with curls going every which way, tangled by waves in opposing channels, and Corcoran almost blurted out, "Shaggy Hair."

"Hello," she said, walking to her desk and taking Dancing Antelope's offered hand. "Who have we here? A new student?" She laughed and stood in front of Corcoran who simply stared into those warm and enticing eyes. She thought, I hope you are a student, mister; I could sure teach you a thing or two. My, my.

"Shaggy Hair, meet my friend, Terrence Corcoran. He's here to get Nate Coppersmith's ranch back for him. I thought you should know each other."

"We should, indeed. How do you do, Mr. Corcoran? I'm Betsy Schultz but my Indian friends have decided that Shaggy Hair is how I'm called." She had a delightful little laugh and offered her hand. Her eyes were not demure; they were flashing bright, right into Corcoran's.

"My pleasure, ma'am," Corcoran said, taking her hand and getting a strong grasp. "Dancing Antelope tells me you and Susan Coppersmith were good friends." *Oh, my. Those eyes are magnificent. I would've ridden ten thousand miles to meet this critter called Shaggy Hair.*

"I have living quarters back through the door there," she said. "Let's go get a pot of coffee going and have a nice chat, shall we? I made fresh bread this morning and I believe Sarah Pine Crow brought in some fresh goat cheese."

At the table, mugs filled with boiling coffee and plates with bread, jam, cheese, and smoked meat in front of them,

Betsy asked the only question raised. "Just how do you plan to get Nate's ranch back?"

During the answer, Betsy learned that Corcoran carried a badge, that his eyes were the brightest green she'd ever seen, and his smile equaled the sky in warmth. She had already met men before who were quick with their wit, fast with their words, and easy on her eyes. This one had all of that and a measure of sincerity that wasn't in the others. She had to fight to take her eyes from his and then only to admire his long, flowing curls and waves of deep reddish hair.

"What would bring an angel to the vast Nevada desert?" he asked.

"Angel is it? No, Mr. Corcoran, no angels around here. Just children who need an education. What's your immediate plan?"

"Dancing Antelope is going to get me hired and I'm going to get rid of Curly Joe. As I said, I'll have to play it by ear after I get an idea of the men I'm facing."

"I think before Dancing Antelope takes you to the ranch to meet this vile Curly Joe Simpson, I'll take you north ten miles or so to meet someone else. The two of you will get along rather well. We'll leave in an hour. Dancing Antelope, ride back to the ranch and tell that man you've found a good cowman to work the ranch. God knows Simpson isn't one."

CHAPTER SIX

"You could have told me who your father was, you know."

"And spoil all the fun? No, Mr. Corcoran, I wanted to see the look on your face." She was looking straight into his big green eyes, smiling like the cat that got away with everything, even gave the slightest bit of a laugh before dropping her gaze.

He was impressed with the way she was able to play with him; her ability to enchant was rooted somewhere deep in her soul and she used those powers effectively. *She's a force to be dealt with, I'm afraid. A quick mind, somewhat devious, and filled with romanticism.* Corcoran wasn't aware that he was describing himself as much as Shaggy Hair. *Lovely ladies that tease, not to gain monetarily but to enchant and accomplish a goal are more than invigorating. She's deliciously devious.*

The ride north was only five miles to the Grant County, Oregon Sheriff's Office and a meeting with David P. Schultz, Sheriff. It had been a quiet ride, Corcoran wondering just what this most attractive white woman who the natives called Shaggy Hair had in mind. During the discussion about coming north to meet someone, she and Dancing Antelope seemed to be sharing a secret of some kind and he wasn't invited to the party.

"How long have you been living in that little village?"

"Almost from its inception," she said. "After what they are calling the Bannock War, the Shoshone, Northern Paiute, and other tribes decided they wanted a village where they could live in peace. The army was called on to help and, so far, we're not infected by other federal agents."

Corcoran had to laugh at that comment. "I like that. Other than the army, are you getting any help?"

"No. I think that's a blessing but there are some, many actually, that want the area to be a mixed reservation for Shoshone and Paiute. That would bring considerable federal interference sometimes called help."

They both laughed as they rode across the imaginary border between Nevada and Oregon and into a small but active ranching community. The Great Basin included most of Nevada, great portions of eastern Oregon, southern Idaho, and was covered in high plains grasses, sage, piñon pine, scrub cedar, and rabbit brush. It took many acres to keep a cow well fed, and there were many ranchers doing their best to raise well-fed cattle.

When Betsy Schultz drew her horse up to the hitching rack in front of the sheriff's office and dismounted, Corcoran was still at a loss as to her purpose. When they walked in the door and she said, "Hi, Dad," he knew he was being duped into something.

Introductions were made and the three settled at a table near a potbelly stove that was almost red hot. "That last storm brought some mighty cold air with it," Schultz said, setting large mugs about. He also produced a flask filled with some fine bourbon. "So, Corcoran, you're a deputy from Eureka County, eh? You're about as far out of your jurisdiction as you could get."

Corcoran chuckled, adding some hefty flavor from the flask to his coffee. "Yup, you could sure say that. Tryin' to help a friend so, right now, just Terrence Corcoran, saddle tramp looking for a job."

"Terrence is here to put things right for Nate and Susan Coppersmith, Dad," Betsy said.

"Good, that needs to be done, sooner than later. Nate's a good man and doesn't need to be treated this way. I got this poster several days ago, Corcoran," he said. He pulled a broad sheet up with pictures of Curly Joe Simpson, Slant Eyed Tom O'Neil, and Rocky Rockefeller. "If I have one, old Peters is sure to have one. Are you working for him?"

"No, Sheriff, I'm not. As far as I know, and from what Coppersmith told me, the Humboldt County Sheriff isn't interested in helping the man out. Peters has some kind of standing grudge against Nate from what I gathered."

"I remember the incident. Old range cow had a young one that needed some doctoring and Nate said as soon as he got a rope on the old girl, Peters could get to the calf. Peters is a hardheaded fool sometimes and he just jumped off the damn horse before Nate could stop him.

"You know mama cows, Corcoran. She wasn't about to let some buckaroo have his way with her calf and pounded that man something fierce. Of course, in Peters' mind, it was all Nate's fault. Damn fool, if you ask me."

Corcoran saw a dedicated lawman who was also worried about a friend and decided immediately that he could trust and work with this Sheriff Schultz. He also was well aware that he could and would spend considerable time with the lovely Shaggy Hair, daughter of said sheriff.

"Carrying a badge doesn't mean bein' a selective law-dog, Sheriff," Corcoran said.

"Nope, doesn't. Call me David." Schultz got up and brought the coffee pot to the table for refills. "Badge carries

a responsibility far bigger than a man's grudges. I'd arrest
Betsy here if she done something horrible." He gave her a
sidelong look, held it for a couple of seconds, like maybe he
was giving it some thought. He chuckled, then broke into a
wry little smile. "Not in her to do something horrible,
though.

"You got some kind of plan to get this Curly Joe Simpson
off that ranch?"

Before Corcoran could tell him about his plan, Shaggy
Hair said that, "Yes, Dad, Susan Coppersmith and I had a
plan. That's why I brought Corcoran to you."

Terrence had a big old dumb look on his face, staring at
Betsy first and then her father. "First I've heard of this," he
mumbled.

"I'm sure of that," Schultz answered. "Well, okay, Betsy,
let's hear what you and Susan have cooked up, then Mr.
Corcoran and I will discuss his plan." He gave Corcoran a
look that said something to the effect of, we'd better do this
or else.

Betsy Schultz huffed twice, once for the Grant County
Sheriff and once for the Eureka County deputy, drank a gulp
of coffee and spelled out her plan which was so simple it
would probably work.

"By damn," Schultz said.

"Son of a gun," Corcoran snuffed.

"Thank you," Betsy said.

Within the hour, Terrence and Betsy were mounting up
for the ride back to her village in Nevada. That's when
Corcoran said, "You might have told me who your
father was."

The few miles back to the village was a bit more animated
than the earlier ride out. "So you think my plan will work?"

Betsy asked, her eyes shining in the midday light, her smile adding to the open range brightness.

They came to a fork in the road and Betsy said, "The right fork leads to the main trail to the Sleepy U ranch. It's a long ride from the ranch to Dad's office but you might want to keep it in mind."

Corcoran laughed and gave his horse a nudge, getting both horses into a trot. What she and Susan Coppersmith had come up with was almost brilliant and he heard Betsy's father come right out and say so. *It's tough enough that I have to spend all this time with this charming lass and not in a romantic situation. Now I have to admit that she is probably going to get Nate's ranch back.*

"Your plan fits right in with what I had in my hard old head," Corcoran said. He was going to save what little face he had left no matter what. "I haven't met this Ephraim Peters yet but I can almost guarantee that I won't like him. You know, I shot one sheriff I worked for."

Betsy took in a quick breath, then giggled at the comment. "Peters is a hard man, Terrence, not like my dad." She looked for a long time at the big man with the flowing almost reddish hair and massive moustache and decided that she was going to enjoy getting to know him just a little bit better.

"How come it is you working for the Indians and all?" he asked.

"I'm a teacher and they needed one. It works out fine."

"I don't like the idea of the county sheriff not doing his duty because of a personal grudge," Corcoran continued. "The more I think about it the more I don't like it. He should bring a deputy or two, ride onto the ranch, and arrest those men. But I do like the plan we're gonna be working on. It will work, Betsy. It will."

"That's a pretty nice horse you ride, Mr. Corcoran. Can he

run?" She laughed and spurred her young mare into a full wide-out gallop, and Corcoran let Rube have full rein, eating dust for some time. They were almost abreast, hooves pounding desert dust into billows behind them when they pulled back into a walk.

"Nice ride, ma'am," is all he said, giving her a smile. "Little mare's got some go in her. I've had old Rube here for fourteen years and you just gave him one of his best runs. I suppose now you'll tell me you breed horses on the side. That is, when you're not too busy making plans to rescue a family's ranch or teaching the Paiute nation's children."

Betsy laughed and flicked her quirt at Corcoran, teasing him just a bit. "Dancing Antelope, Nate Coppersmith, and I have been discussing the possibility. I have this little girl's sire and dam, and two other breeding mares already."

"I'll be damned," is all Corcoran could say. *Well, by golly, I will be damned. I have to know a whole lot more about this fine lady. I've never wanted to be a cattle rancher, ever. But breeding and training horses? Oh, my.* Corcoran's mind was alive and working the rest of the ride.

The typical afternoon wind had come up and with it problems for Betsy Schultz. He laughed watching her try to control the mass of unruly hair by first trying to tie it back, then putting on a scarf, and finally just slamming her hat down as tight as it would go. "Thus, we have Shaggy Hair, teacher of Paiutes and Shoshone children." She couldn't help herself and laughed right along with him.

Dancing Antelope met them about a mile out from the village. "Simpson fool say to bring you to him, Corcoran. He don't know much about cows so he not gonna ask very smart questions to you."

"Good, Dancing Antelope. Good. We'll gather my kit at

my little camp and ride into the Sleepy U. You okay riding the rest of the way into the village by yourself, Shaggy Hair?" he asked and chuckled.

"Go do your duty, Mr. Corcoran," she snapped. Then she smiled, "And I'll see you for supper on Saturday."

"Yes, ma'am," he said, touched his heels to Rube, and he and Dancing Antelope rode off at a lope. Dinner on Saturday? Anything you say, Betsy Schultz.

She rode into the village with visions of bright green eyes, long flowing curls of reddish blond hair, and tall tales dancing in her mind. He shot a sheriff?

"You don't look quite as happy as you did." Corcoran and the Paiute were moving along at a brisk lope, eating up miles of Nevada high desert. "Something I should know?"

"Yup. Be very careful of this fool Simpson. He killed the only man that knew anything about cows, that one they called Slant Eye. Other feller, this one called Rocky Feller, he dumb as chicken but as dangerous as lion," he laughed and said. "Gonna be big fight getting Simpson off ranch."

Corcoran had visions of a dumb dangerous chicken as he packed his mule and they made good time riding the short distance from his campsite into the headquarters of the Sleepy U. Simpson was standing on the veranda-style porch watching them ride in. "Don't unpack that mule until we talk," he snarled and stalked back into the big house.

"Friendly sort," Corcoran murmured. He tied his animals off and headed for the house. "Coming?"

"No," Dancing Antelope said. "Gonna find Rocky Feller and see if he can rope a fence post." He rode off laughing softly, pretending to build a loop.

Corcoran found Curly Joe Simpson in the kitchen pouring

whiskey into a glass. He did not offer any. "Sit down. You a cow man?"

Corcoran was looking at a rooster, dressed in linen finery, clean and pressed. That vision of a dangerous chicken simply wouldn't go away. Simpson wasn't a big man by Corcoran's standards and he knew he could take him physically in an instant. He saw a big Colt tucked in his waist and wondered where the knife might be. *Except for what I read on that poster I don't know nothin' about Curly Joe Simpson. Dancing Antelope said he shot Slant Eye but I don't know nothin' about him either.*

"For many years, Simpson. Saw part of your herd ridin' in. Looks like you'll have a good calf crop come spring."

"Pay's a dollar a day and food."

Simpson ain't no cowman. A good one would have jumped on my comment with a hearty thank you and a smile. Just a common dumb outlaw here. Corcoran let a little smile crease his face.

"That's a bit thin, ain't it?" Corcoran wanted to push the man just a little bit, see what kind of reaction he might get. "Used to just a bit more."

"That's what it is," Simpson barked. "Take it or ride out. Ain't got time to argue. Your call. Don't like it, ride out."

"Difference between takin' and likin'," Corcoran said. "I'll take it. Who's the ramrod?"

"For the time being, the Indian. He knows the ranch, the range, and the herd. You'll be working with Rocky Rockefeller. Bunkhouse is over there. There's a stove; you're on your own for cookin'. There's flour, cornmeal, coffee, and bacon. Want anything else, you find it."

Corcoran walked out to his horse and mule and headed toward the bunkhouse. "He should name the ranch slim pickin's," he murmured. "So Dancing Antelope's days are numbered and this Rocky is the third man on the poster. Walk soft, Mr. Corcoran, walk soft."

David Schultz stood in the doorway of his little office watching his daughter and Terrence Corcoran ride out into the high desert. "He's looking for outlaws and she's lookin' for him." He chuckled. "You better be one tough hombre, Corcoran." He walked across the narrow street, now a sea of mud in the noon-time sun. His aim was to the Golden Gulch Saloon for a cold beer and talk with his part-time deputy, Standish Brown.

"Mornin' Brownie. A frosty glassed cold one would make my mornin' complete."

"How do, David. Was that Betsy rode in with a cowboy?" He pulled a mug out of a bucket of ice and pulled the tap from a big keg, shoving a foamy mug of homemade brew across the bar.

The Golden Gulch was situated in a long but not wide two-story building. It shared the first floor with a barbershop and the second floor held two apartments, one of which was rented by Mr. Brown. The barber rented the other and David Schultz owned the building and the saloon.

"When was the last time you pushed a cow around, Brownie?"

"I guess last spring at some of the brandings. What's up?" Stan Brown was straight up from southern California's Spanish ranches, learned to ride from his Mexican mother's brothers and cousins, and looked more like a Spanish Vaquero when he rode than an American cowman.

"That man riding with Betsy is a lawman from Eureka County, Nevada. He's gonna throw those bums that are trying to steal Coppersmith's ranch out the door and he might just need a bit of help. Any of those jokers been up here? Have any of them seen you?"

"I saw the poster on them and I ain't seen any one of 'em around here. You say this dude riding' with Betsy is from way down in Eureka County? Couldn't get much more out of his jurisdiction."

Schultz laughed, drank some beer, his eyes shining brightly at the thought of jurisdiction. "Where did all that come from, Brownie? Jurisdiction? Hell, we're all lawmen, we all try to uphold the same laws." He paused thinking of Pete Peters. "Well, some of us do."

"Territorial jealousy, David. Can't let someone else uphold the law in your territory. It's yours to uphold. It's also childish but it's also the way we do things." He chuckled. "It's also too damn early for this kind of talk. Whew. Philosophy and cold beer." He had to chuckle as he poured another mug for the sheriff. "You obviously have something cooking."

"Yeah, I do, Brownie. I want you to ride down to the Sleepy U and find either Dancing Antelope or Terrence Corcoran and join in as a ranch hand."

"Corcoran? That was Terrence Corcoran riding with Betsy? Is she okay?" He had a strange look on his face, like maybe he ate a lemon or a green persimmon. "Corcoran's always been a good lawman, David, but around a pretty girl like Betsy? Oh, my."

"I'm gonna worry more about him than I am Betsy." Schultz laughed. "You should have seen her eyes when she looked at him. He's in more trouble than he knows. And, yes, I want you to ride with him and Dancing Antelope on the ranch. We're gonna bust those outlaws off Nate Coppersmith's ranch and soon."

Schultz told him how Peters would not do his duty and arrest Simpson, would not help his former employer, and how Corcoran was acting alone with no jurisdiction or back up. "Those men need to be taken out, Brownie, and you and Corcoran are the ones to do it. I'll get Stony to run the bar.

"And by the way, you are not acting as a sheriff's deputy in any way. You're just helping out a good friend in need. We'll catch hell from everybody if we're not careful."

Brownie shook his head, a wry grin forming slowly. "If this ain't something. A Nevada deputy out of his jurisdiction working with an Indian who has no jurisdiction and helped by an Oregon deputy out of his jurisdiction. A judge might just have a lot of fun with this, David."

"If we're lucky, there won't be any judges getting involved in any way. We can't take a chance on Peters finding out what we're doing either. That fool would throw a horseshoe in the middle just to spite old Nate Coppersmith. When can you leave?"

"Won't take an hour to get put together. Just ride right up to the ranch?"

"No. You need to talk to Corcoran or Dancing Antelope first. They'll bring you up to speed on what we're doing. We gotta do this right, Brownie."

CHAPTER SEVEN

It was mid-afternoon when Brownie neared the Sleepy U ranch and was intercepted by Dancing Antelope. "Hey, Brown Man. Ha! Now I got a Rocky Feller and a Brown Man. White mans have funny names cuz you ain't brown and he ain't a rock."

"And you ain't an antelope," Brownie replied and laughed. "Schultz wants you to get me a job on this ranch. I'm gonna work with you and Corcoran to get these hombres under lock and key. Tell me about this Curly Joe Simpson."

It was a good hour's ride into the ranch and Dancing Antelope described Simpson and all but dismissed Rockefeller except to mention that he considered the man stupid but dangerous. Lights were already burning in the kitchen of Coppersmith's big house when they rode up. Simpson came out on the porch with a shotgun.

"Hey, Curly Joe, don't shoot, it's me," Dancing Antelope said. "Got you another good cowman. Known him long time, works good. Meet Stan Brown."

"Come in and talk, Brown," is all Simpson said walking back into the kitchen.

Dancing Antelope and Corcoran were in the barn when Brownie joined them. "I think we can talk here. Rocky Feller having big talk with Simpson. Brownie work for Schultz, Terrence, and now we all work together."

"David didn't go into a lot of detail, Corcoran. Just what is this big play of ours?"

Corcoran chuckled, reached out and whacked Brown across the back and shoulders. "Brownie, I haven't seen you since we penned up that bunch in Idaho two or three years ago. I heard the leader of the fools is out and lookin' for us."

"Heard the same thing, Terrence. Bronco Johnny Ladd. You're right, leader of the fools."

"Well, we got another one just inside the doors over there. There were three but Simpson wiped out his best man. We need to entice these fools in some way to get them across the state line and into Oregon. Local sheriff is a zero, I've got no jurisdiction, but David Schultz does if we can get them into Oregon.

"One thing that's been bothering me more and more is the possibility of Simpson working in cahoots with either the land agent or Sheriff Peters, or maybe both. This is too sweet a deal; happened too quickly for there not being some kind of help along the way.

"And," he took a pause to make sure there wasn't anyone nearby. "The fool should have sold the ranch before this. For this kind of land fraud to work, the exchange has to be quick. What I'm saying is, we need to be as quick as possible getting them into Oregon."

"Good plan," Brownie said. "The idea of Peters being involved is probably out of the question. As much as he hates Coppersmith, he's not smart enough to involve himself. That

Reg Chapman, though...," and Brown took a long pause. "He's slippery as snake oil. As I said, I like the plan."

"Don't know how that help Nate," Dancing Antelope said. "They still have place. Why not just shoot the two men and send note to Nate."

"This is one of those white man and property things, Dancing Antelope. Just as Curly Joe said that Nate abandoned his claim, when these idiots are in custody they will have abandoned their claim. Not too complicated, but I'm sure someone from some government agency will make it so." Corcoran squatted down and fished a cigar from his shirt pocket. "That's our entire plan, Brownie."

"Really gone into detail, Corcoran." He laughed. "What do we know about this Rockefeller? I've never heard of him until the broadsheet came in. Bank jobs, murder, cattle rustling, from Texas all the way through to Arizona. They've been busy boys." Brown walked around the barn a bit, nodding from time to time. "You don't really think Peters is involved, do you?"

"The thought's had a fling, Brownie. Same with the land agent. Doesn't make sense, though. If they were, wouldn't Simpson be trying to sell this place? Why, with paper out on him, is he trying to keep it?"

"Stupid," is all Brownie said, getting nods from Dancing Antelope and Corcoran.

"What are you men talking about?" It was Simpson and Rockefeller coming into the barn.

"Dancing Antelope is giving us a run-down on the ranch operations," Corcoran said. "I like the way you've got the cattle down for the winter. Seems like a few head have been left up in the rocks, though. We'll get them choused out soon enough."

"You better if you want to keep working for this brand,"

Simpson snarled. "Rocky, you ride with Corcoran tomorrow and, Brown, you ride with the injun."

"Name's Dancing Antelope," the injun said with emphasis. Simpson whuffed a couple of times, his eyes narrowed and shoulders braced.

It didn't go past that and Simpson never saw Corcoran and Brownie flex their fingers toward some big iron. He turned and walked out, telling the men to get some sleep and start early as if no cowboy ever needed more sleep or didn't get up before the sun anyway. "Sure, boss," Rockefeller said getting snickers from Corcoran and Brownie.

"Come on, Rocky, get your butt in gear. We've got cattle to move." Corcoran had Rube saddled and was ready to ride while Rockefeller was still trying to catch his horse. The sky was already blanched and starting to turn pink in areas. Rockefeller made another loop and missed his throw again. Dancing Antelope and Brownie were already on the trail, taking the north circle this day.

"Don't be talkin' to me that way. I ain't workin' for you."

"You ain't workin' is what I see. You and Simpson pretty tight are you?"

"What's that supposed to mean? We been ridin' together for a long time."

"Yeah," Corcoran said. Rockefeller finally caught his horse up, saddled him, and they rode out to the south to bring the strays out of the high mountains surrounding the valley. "Hope some of that ridin' had something to do with cattle." Corcoran knew this was the man he watched bring part of the herd down a few days ago. Must have learned to ride a horse from running away from posses but he sure didn't know nothing about cattle.

"We gotta take a break," Rocky said about two hours into their circle. "We're pushing too hard."

"We ain't started pushing hard," Corcoran sneered. "You gonna be working this herd for old Simpson, you better get your learning cap on. You don't ride up hard on a cow or small group, and you don't go yellin' and hollerin' either. You 'bout spooked the whole bunch we got.

"Now, you either do it my way or, buster, get the hell away from what I'm doing." Corcoran snorted, smacked his coiled lariat against his chaps, and spit. "You are not a cowman."

"You better not keep talking to me that way, Corcoran." Rockefeller was big and strong, dumb as the day is long, and wanted to shoot the Irisher on the spot. Corcoran was hoping he would try.

"What are you gonna do?" Corcoran sneered. "Tell Simpson that I made you do a day's work? Ooh, big man gonna tell on me? This used to be a good brand to ride for, Rocky, but you ain't up to it, boy."

"Don't you ever call me boy," Rockefeller screamed, turning in the saddle, his revolver in hand but only for half a second. That heavy coil of lariat swished across Rocky's face and down, jerking the pistol out of his grip. He howled at the burn on his face, forgetting he even once held a gun.

"I wonder if you'll tell the so-called big man that you drew on me, Rocky? Somehow I

doubt that he would be pleased to know that you aren't quite the man you think you are."

Corcoran stepped off his horse and picked up the weapon, blowing dust out of the workings, and tucked it into his belt.

"I'll just keep this until we get back. Now, get your butt moving and let's get this beef down to the winter feeding grounds."

Rockefeller spent the next eight to ten hours seething, letting his anger come close to boiling over, wanting to kill this big man talking down to him. Corcoran never let Rocky get behind him, even when the fool got tangled up in his own lariat. Corcoran tied off his reata so his right hand would always be free to pull the Colt if needed.

Once again, Dancing Antelope had his cattle down in the winter range near the pond half an hour before Corcoran and Rocky rode in with theirs. "What happened to you? You fall off your horse?" Dancing Antelope was pointing at the bright red marks on Rockefeller's face.

"Shut up, injun," Rockefeller snarled, jerking his horse's head around and spurring hard for a fast ride back to the corrals.

"What'd you do, Corcoran?" Brownie had a grin on his face.

"Simpson said to learn him something about working cows." Corcoran smiled, putting Rube in a gentle lope back to the barns. He could hear Dancing Antelope and Brownie laughing and joshing most of the way. There was no sign of Rocky when they got back. I'm sure I'll hear about it, he thought; I would sure like to hear the explanation for the rope burns and the fact he's managed to lose his sidearm. Dancing Antelope was right, though. The man was stupid and dangerous.

"Bacon and biscuits ain't the best meal I've had," Brownie said, setting his plate down and joining Corcoran. Dancing Antelope went back to his own camp and said he'd probably ride into the village tomorrow. "Wonder what Simpson's having?"

"Probably eatin' off one of his best steers." Corcoran chuckled. "He'd never think to slaughter a cull. What I'm wondering is what that fool Rocky told him about his face. I've been expecting a visit since we got back."

"Yup," is all Brownie said. He put more wood in the stove and brought the coffee pot to the table. "You got kind of a plan worked up on how to get these jaspers up to Grant County?"

"Hopin' you might," Corcoran responded. "We need some excuse for all of us to leave the ranch; not go to the Indian village but go to Grant County. Maybe a fall fair? Maybe a rodeo? Something that would draw an outlaw like Simpson away from here."

Brownie didn't have time to answer the questions when the door to the bunkhouse flew open and Rockefeller and Simpson strode in. "What the hell happened out there today, Corcoran? What did you do to Rocky?" There was wild fury in the man's eyes, his fists were clenched and his neck was bowed.

"Kept the man from shootin' me, Simpson. You wanted me to help him learn the ways of cattle and all he did was want to be a cry-baby." He watched Rockefeller tense like a mountain lion coming on a spring lamb and wondered if this would be the end of the Curly Joe Simpson gang. "Told him what to do and he pulled a gun on me." He got a half smile across his rugged face. "I forgot to give that back to you, Rocky. Want it now?" He thought about reaching for the revolver still tucked in his waistband but didn't.

"Ain't the story I heard," Simpson snarled.

"That means Rocky Feller there is a liar," Corcoran said, mimicking Dancing Antelope.

Simpson didn't have time to say anything before Rockefeller lunged at Corcoran, knocking Simpson aside. Rockefeller outweighed Corcoran by a bit but Corcoran was far faster and considerably stronger.

He took the lunge and used the extra energy from it to roll back and throw Rockefeller up against the wall. He jumped to his feet and pasted the big outlaw with a left straight out of his shoulder breaking the man's nose and followed that up with a driving right into Rocky's heart. Rocky couldn't breathe, his nose was a bloody geyser, and Corcoran stood stock-still, grinned at Brownie, and brought a left roundhouse that took Rockefeller across the room and left him crumpled on the floor.

"If you've got nothin' else, Simpson, me and Brownie haven't had supper yet."

Simpson hauled Rockefeller to his feet and the two high-tailed it back to the ranch house. "You two make that herd ready for winter," is all he said. Corcoran snickered and fondled Rockefeller's pistol still stuck in his waistband.

"He whupped on you pretty good," Simpson said when they got settled in the kitchen. He had a bottle of whiskey on the table and two cups.

"He'll be dead in the morning."

"We need to do some thinking, Rocky. Some hard thinking. I'm wondering if maybe Slant Eyed Tom might have been right. Maybe we ought to sell this place and get out of this country. We're better at bank jobs than we are at cows." He had to chuckle at his thoughts.

Rocky only had revenge in his thoughts. "Don't give a damn 'bout anything but that man bein' dead."

"What was that man's name in the village that we were supposed to sell this ranch to? What was it? He was like an Indian agent or maybe trader? Damn." Simpson watched Rockefeller storm around the kitchen, trying to remember the man's name. This had all been put together and now Simpson was in a pickle. He was supposed to have met with the man months ago.

"He weren't no Indian agent, Curly Joe," Rocky said. "He has a ranch up in Oregon and said his name was Peabody."

"Yeah, that's it. Henry Peabody. You and me're ridin' into that village in the morning to see if we can find that man. He said he did business with the Indians all the time." Simpson poured each of them another full mug of whiskey. "Get yourself cleaned up, Rocky. We'll ride out at first light."

CHAPTER EIGHT

"What do you suppose those two are really up to?" Brownie was putting a loop on his horse in the corral watching Curly Joe Simpson and Rockefeller ride out. "You sure put some lumps on that man's head, Corcoran."

"Felt damn good doin' it, too. Only thing worse than a mouthy outlaw is a law-dog gone sour. I'm gonna see those two in prison and I'm gonna personally remove the badge from Mr. Peters. The more I think about what's going on with Nate Coppersmith and his family, the more angry I get."

He cinched the saddle down good and mounted Rube. "Whatever it is they're working on, I'll guarantee we get in the middle of it." They laughed some. "Let's work some cows and see if we can figure out a way to get those yahoos into Grant County."

"A fair or rodeo wouldn't work on them, Terrence. They ain't buckaroos and they ain't ranchers. They are outlaws, so what would catch the attention of bank robbers and murderers?"

They were riding in beautiful country, slopes leading out of the long wide valley into steep rocky formations where old steers and cows could evade detection for years. The sky was endless, the late fall temperature was perfect for working hard, and the work of chasing cattle out of high country was invigorating.

"I could eat a buffalo right now, Brownie." They just deposited another twenty-five or so head of older cows near the pond. "Let's ride back to the ranch and see what Curly Joe has in his kitchen."

"Steak, taters, and a touch of bourbon to wash it down, and I'll bet Simpson has all that waiting for us to take. I won't arrest you if you won't arrest me." Brownie grinned.

"Out of my jurisdiction," is all Corcoran said.

They laughed and joshed most of the way back, did a bit of racing, Rube proving once again that he was as much a cow horse as a racing pony, and they were still carousing some as they walked into the kitchen. "Fool didn't even leave a good fire. Well, we'll get it stoked up some."

"We got company, Terrence," Brownie said. They pulled their weapons and stood near the stove as someone ran across the porch and slammed into the kitchen. If this was Simpson and Rockefeller coming back from the village, there would be hell to pay, them being in the ranch house and all.

Simpson and Rockefeller rode into the little village still being built. There were wickiups, teepees, and wood frame buildings sharing space; Indians building their new homes and soldiers from Fort McDermott either helping or watching. It was a busy little village, filled with children and dogs running in every direction, and people trying to get through the day.

"Where would I find Henry Peabody?" Curly Joe asked one of the soldiers standing along the main street.

"Don't know the man," he said. "Might want to ask at the

trading post down that way," he said, pointing off down the street.

Simpson didn't bother to nod or say thank you, just nudged his horse down the street. "We'll buy a bottle of good whiskey, Rocky, and get Peabody juiced some, then make us a good deal."

"All I want to do is ride back to the ranch and kill Corcoran." Rockefeller's face burned from the whipping he took from the rope and his nose was more than painful. He had a black eye and his upper lip was split and still bleeding.

"You can do that after we make the deal with Peabody."

They tied their horses off in front of a walled tent structure that said Fort Henry Trading Post but the word Henry was crossed off. There were tables and racks spread around inside and out filled with the kind of merchandise that would be needed in a building village. Simpson pushed his way past a couple of Indian women getting into the store, followed by Rocky.

"Well, Mr. Simpson, I believe. Welcome to my little enterprise." Henry Peabody was a tall thin man, probably around fifty or so, sporting a long white beard and equally long white hair tied back Indian style. He wore canvas trousers and a mountain man style buckskin pullover shirt. His arms and legs seemed extraordinarily long despite his tall stature.

"I hope you're here to discuss me buying that Sleepy U ranch of yours. According to our friend, you were supposed to be here some time ago. I understand you're looking at a good spring calf crop."

"That's why we're here, Peabody. Got some place we can talk?"

"I have my living quarters in the back," he said. "Chasing Rabbits, will you watch the store for a few minutes?" The young Indian girl, probably fourteen or slightly older, nodded with a beautiful smile. Peabody led the men into the back where they could sit at a comfortable table.

Rockefeller nudged Simpson as they walked past the young girl and had a definite leer on his wounded face. "Nice," he whispered. "Might enjoy something like that." Simpson just growled and kept walking.

"Would you gentlemen like something a little stronger than coffee? I have the pleasure of offering some real Kentucky bourbon that arrived just this week." He reached up and took a jug from a shelf and put it on the table. "This will bring pictures of rolling Kentucky hills filled with tall horses," he said and laughed.

Simpson sneered and he and Rocky sat down while Peabody filled the cups already on the table. "Wouldn't normally ask, but those rope burns look like they might get infected," Peabody said to Rocky. "We have a lovely lady here in the village who takes care of those of us get hurt or sick. Would you like her to take a look?"

Rockefeller wasn't sure what to say, gulped down about half a mug of whiskey and looked to Simpson to say something. "Got hurt workin' some cattle yesterday, Peabody. Wouldn't hurt for someone to look at him, though. He's a tough one, Rocky is, but infection in this country is bad."

Rockefeller looked away from Simpson's lie and let his eyes roam out toward the front of the trading post. He was fully engrossed in watching Chasing Rabbits helping customers out front, unaware he was still being talked about. The last time he'd felt a woman close to him was before the bank job in Austin. She was in a buckskin dress wearing moccasins that came half way up her calf and he could see every curve, bump, and move she made.

Peabody walked back out to the front of the store to send someone out and came right back. "She'll be here shortly." He took a healthy drink of whiskey and smiled at the two. "Did you have some figure in mind for that ranch of yours, Simpson? Looks to be a standard homestead of a quarter section." Peabody was well aware of what he was going to pay, knew the ranch intimately, and was talking in case someone else might be listening.

Curly Joe remembered the land agent using that same phrase and nodded. "That's right. I'm open to a reasonable offer at this point, Peabody. We kind of fell into having this and don't really want it," he lied.

"I'd be willing to go two dollars an acre at this point. Most of the property around here sells for less but you have those natural ponds and some good winter grazing land that most don't have."

"Seems kinda thin, Peabody."

"Well, of course, we haven't counted in the cattle and sheep, or the hogs and buildings

yet. That's just the land," he said. Peabody's eyes were bright and his smile never wavered. The man was a born trader and Simpson was sure he was gonna play out this deal right to the end.

He had no idea the value of such things. Give the man a chance to look at a bank for a few days and he could tell you within a few hundred dollars how much he would take out of it, but how much was an acre of land? How much was a cow worth? Or a barn? "Give me a complete figure, Peabody, and I'll tell you yes or no."

Peabody smiled, sitting back in his chair. His figure on the land was fair but he was gonna steal the cattle and sheep and give virtually nothing for the big house and the outbuildings. That was the deal. Then he could sell it for a good profit and all three would benefit. He poured some more whiskey around the table, still smiling, his eyes still bright and friendly. He was about to say something when Betsy Schultz walked up to the table.

"Betsy," he said, jumping to his feet. "So glad you could make it. We have an injured man here." She could only see the backs of Simpson and Rockefeller and stepped around the table to shake hands with Henry Peabody. She didn't want to be there in the first place. Peabody was a thief in her opinion, cheating the local Indians, buying ranches for far less than their value simply because the rancher was in financial straits.

When she turned to greet the visitors she gasped, jumping back and around Peabody. "You!" She pointed at Curly Joe. "You vile man, you thief, scoundrel," she shouted.

She turned to Peabody. "These are the men who stole the ranch from Nate Coppersmith." She pointed her finger at Simpson. "That's Curly Joe Simpson. He's wanted for bank robbery and murder, and that's James Rockefeller, a known murderer. They are wanted men." She was talking loud and fast, people from the front of the trading post were paying attention, and the girl, Chasing Rabbits walked back to see if she could help.

"Shut up, woman!" Rockefeller shouted, jumping up from the table. He took a big step toward Betsy and she turned and bolted around Peabody, looking to run out of the front of the store. Simpson stepped in front of her and tried to grab her.

Peabody said, "No," and pushed Simpson away. "What's all this about? I thought you said you owned that ranch?" He had to play the part of trader, not ranch thief. "What do you mean, Betsy? He stole it?" He only heard that part of what she'd said; the murder and bank robber part hadn't cleared yet. "You said the homestead was legal and honest. What are you men trying to pull here?"

Betsy Schultz was trapped behind the table at the far back of the trading post, trying to hide behind Henry Peabody. "They're wanted men, Henry. They're bank robbers and murderers. Help me!" she screamed just as Rockefeller pushed the table aside.

He reached out and shoved Peabody out of the way. The tall thin man tried to fight back but a heavy fist crushed the side of this head and he sprawled onto the hard-packed dirt floor. People up front were yelling for help, hoping that the soldiers would come to Betsy's rescue.

Rockefeller grabbed her by her wild hair and slammed a fist into her face, knocking her unconscious. He flung her to the ground and was about to kick her in the head when Simpson grabbed him. "Let's go. We gotta get out of here now, Rocky." They ran for the front of the trading post just as a soldier stepped in, his revolver in hand.

Simpson's gun was out instantly and one quick shot took the soldier to the ground. Rocky grabbed Chasing Rabbits and the men used her as a shield as they quickly made their way to the horses. Simpson rode hard and fast, back toward the ranch, Rockefeller right behind him, and Chasing Rabbits screaming for help.

"We can't go back, Rocky, we gotta go north. Get rid of that girl. Throw her away."

"She's mine, Curly Joe. She's our protection." He laughed. They rode hard on the westbound trail hoping to intersect with one heading north into Oregon. If they hadn't made for the ranch first, they would already be on the road to Oregon.

It was chaos in the village. The only semblance of order were the few soldiers there from the fort, many miles to the east. A sergeant was found and brought to the trading post and he dispatched a rider to notify the fort of the shooting of one of their own.

Betsy was sitting on the dirt floor in the back of the trading post, sobbing while Henry Peabody was nursing a split lip and sore ribs. Dancing Antelope arrived about ten minutes after the fracas. "You're sure it was Curly Joe?"

"Oh, yes, I'm sure," she sobbed. There was as much anger

as there was hurt. "That brute Rockefeller did this," she said, nursing her bruised jaw. "Go tell my father, please."

"No," he said gently. "I go get Corcoran and Brown Man. Then we go get Schultz Man." He got her to her feet and watched her gently wipe away the tears. "You stay with my family. Pea Man, you help her."

He walked toward the front of the trading post and started for his horse. "Dancing Antelope," a short and rather heavy Paiute woman said, "those white mans took Chasing Rabbits. Save her, Dancing Antelope. Save my granddaughter!"

"Dancing Antelope," Corcoran stammered when he walked out the kitchen door. "What's the hurry, man?" Dancing Antelope baled off his horse well before it was stopped and raced to the porch.

"Big trouble, Corcoran. That Rocky Feller man beat up Shaggy Hair and kidnapped young girl. You come quick, bring Brown Man. Village need you, Corcoran."

Corcoran and Brownie were saddled and the three were on their way to the village in just minutes. "Tell me the whole story, Dancing Antelope," Corcoran said. They rode at a strong lope but knew they would have to slow it down soon or kill their horses. They'd been riding on cattle all day.

"Look," Corcoran said, pointing at hoof prints leaving the main road from the village. "Two horses moving fast and turning north. You said those men were riding toward the ranch but they didn't get there and you did. These have to be their tracks."

"That means they're riding toward Grant County without our help," Brownie said. "Let's follow along. If they have a young girl hostage, we gotta be careful, very careful."

"Tell me about the attack, Dancing Antelope. Why did

Rockefeller attack Betsy? Is she all right?" Corcoran wanted
to ride to Betsy on the one hand and knew he had to ride to
the outlaws on the other. A kidnapped girl? No, not when he
was around.

"Only saw after it happened, Corcoran. Shaggy Hair got
hit hard but," and he laughed and said, "she always say she got
hard head, so not hurt bad."

"They've got a good lead and we have tired horses. Let's
ride. That little girl needs us and sooner, not later." Corcoran
put the spurs to Rube and Brownie and Dancing Antelope fell
in behind him.

CHAPTER NINE

"You are positive the men who shot the trooper were Curly Joe Simpson and James Rockefeller?" The cavalry lieutenant was young, very handsome in his blue uniform, showing every ounce of social grace ever learned at the academy. "Miss Schultz, tell me again what happened?"

Roland 'Rolly' Buckmaster, late of New York and assigned to Fort McDermott, Nevada as his first duty station following graduation form the Military Academy, was more than taken by the lovely Betsy Schultz despite her injuries. He was standing near the table where Betsy was sitting. Peabody had nursed her wounds and she had nursed his.

Buckmaster was commanding the small detachment in the little village still being built, which consisted of a sergeant, a corporal, and eight enlisted privates. To lose a trooper to an outlaw on his first command was a devastating blow to the young officer. Then, to meet such a charming and lovely young lady in such a frontier situation was wonderful.

She sported a black eye - the bruise quickly turning more than one shade of purple - a broken tooth, and the lump on her jaw was more than evident. None of that bothered her as much as the injury to her pride. "That man knocked me flat on my back end," she squalled, pounding her fist onto the table. "He's not to be allowed to get away with that."

Betsy stood straight, squared her shoulders and looked at the young cavalry officer doing his best not to smile too much. "Before you shoot that foul man, before you hang him for shooting that young soldier, you give him to me for five minutes," she said, almost in a snarl.

"Please," Buckmaster said, "tell me again exactly what happened."

It took less than two minutes for Betsy to tell of the attack and then went into the why of it. "My father is the sheriff of Grant County, Oregon, just a few miles north of here, and he showed me a poster of the men. Curly Joe Simpson and James Rockefeller are wanted men. Wanted for murder and they are bank robbers. They kidnapped little Chasing Rabbits after shooting that poor soldier."

She broke down, sat back down at the table, and could still see Chasing Rabbits screaming as the men rode off. Tears were flowing and Buckmaster found himself leaning down to the beautiful lady with a clean handkerchief. "I'll call for a squad immediately and begin our pursuit, Miss Schultz." He walked to the front of the tent and had his sergeant form up a five-man patrol.

"Peabody said they rode west, Sergeant. Do you have a tracker in this group?"

"Aye, we do, sir," Sergeant Hiram Banion said. "Patrol is ready, sir." The patrol consisted of Lieutenant Buckmaster, Sergeant Banion, four troopers, and a Paiute tracker from the village.

Banion was a product of the Boston docks and joined the army when the War Between the States broke out as a way to be rid of the docks and the environment. He'd been a sergeant three times now and vowed not to lose those stripes ever again no matter how good the whiskey was that was being served.

"Mount up," Buckmaster called. Betsy ran out of the trading post and up to the lieutenant.

"I want to go with you. I know this country better than anyone around here except Dancing Antelope."

"No, ma'am." That's all Buckmaster said, waved his arm, and the group rode off leaving Betsy standing in the roadway, furious that she was left behind. The dust was still in the air from the army patrol riding out of the village as Betsy was fitting a saddle to her pretty little mare.

"They've slowed considerably, Brownie," Corcoran said. "We're more than an hour behind them and it's too dark to see. Let's call it for today, eat what we took from the kitchen, and ride hard tomorrow."

He got no argument from either Brown or Dancing Antelope. "You've been following those tracks with little problem, Dancing Antelope. What about in the dark? Could you still follow?"

"Sure. Easy tracking them two. But these horses pooped," he said.

"I was thinking very early start."

"Sure, Corcoran. Good moon, no wind to cover tracks. Sure. We sleep, horses eat, we go," he said. Brownie had the fire nice and hot, coffee almost boiling, and side meat frying in minutes.

"Probably one, maybe two," Corcoran said when Brownie asked what time it was.

"Feels like I just put my head down," he said. "We moved ten thousand head of cattle and then chased the whole damn

Sioux Nation across the continent yesterday. I need more sleep." He was chuckling to himself as he crawled out of his blanket. "Okay, okay, I'm up."

"Let's get this circus moving. We can stop after sunrise for a quick meal and coffee but we'll get several hours jump on those yahoos."

They were on the trail for two hours when Dancing Antelope veered off toward a stand of piñon pines and a springs several miles away. "Betcha they camped over there," he said.

"We're close," Corcoran said. "They're not half an hour ahead of us. Let's put these fine critters in a good fast trot and see if we can't have them in our sights by sunrise." The moon was giving them enough light that it felt almost like sunrise.

That part of the great basin was mostly flat, broken up by rocky hills, deep gulches, and scrub brush. The trail they were on connected with Burns, Oregon, but Corcoran was almost sure these outlaws would not be riding into Sheriff Schultz's home ground. "They'll be breaking off this trail, Dancing Antelope."

"Yeah, sure," he said. "Shaggy Hair's father up at Burns. Betcha they go east and then north again."

They were moving fast along the trail when Dancing Antelope pulled up to a fast stop. "Look." He was pointing at a slight haze of dust about a mile in front of them. "Not just riders on trail, Corcoran. Something wrong."

The ride out of the village had been fast and hard, Curly Joe Simpson in the lead and Rocky Rockefeller having a hard time staying up while fighting with Chasing Rabbits who was determined to get away from the men. Rockefeller smacked her a couple of times which only made the teenager fight harder.

"Let me go!" she screamed, scratched at his already battered face, kicked him at every opportunity, and vowed to kill the white men at her first chance. Chasing Rabbits was almost five feet and four inches tall, lithe and strong, budding into womanhood, and she was fighting for her life. She had heard terrible stories from the women of the village about how the white men treated Indian women and she was not going to let that happen to her.

Rockefeller made a big mistake when he bent down to grab a fleeting kiss. Chasing Rabbits sunk her teeth in his already broken nose and opened wounds now gushing with hot blood. She spit what went in her mouth in his face and struggled more to get free. A solid whack across the side of her head settled the argument. Curly Joe Simpson chuckled at the whimpering Rockefeller.

"She's your protection?" He laughed. "You got yourself a serious problem, Rocky-Man," he jibed, snickering as he rode hard. "Dump her, you fool."

After half an hour of hard riding, Simpson pulled his horse down into a walk, letting the animal catch its breath. He found what he was looking for, an old trail north, which should take them near Burns and they could then swing east and north, eventually getting into the Snake River Valley. They'd have to go through the Jordan Valley to get there.

"Throw that damn girl off, Rocky. We ain't got time for that kind of nonsense. Get rid of her."

"Naw, I think she likes me, Curly." He laughed, smacked Chasing Rabbits hard to quiet her down. "She'll be good protection."

They rode north for several hours, looking behind often to see if anyone was following,

found a spring off in a stand of pines, off the main trail by a few miles, and made a quick camp. Chasing Rabbits bit Rockefeller in the hand hard enough to show bone where the thumb connected to the wrist when he stepped off his horse and jerked her with him.

"Miserable little bitch," he yelled, knocking her down with a fist to the side of her head. He was holding his hand close to his body trying to get the bleeding under control. "Look what she did." He held his hand out toward Curly Joe who whacked it aside.

"I told you a dozen times to get rid of the girl. Oh, no, you said. She'll protect us. Some protection, Rocky. Now, you're gonna die from bites from a filthy injun. Stupid!" He swung a mighty right from way behind his back knocking the bigger man flat on his face. "You kick her out of this camp right now or I'm gonna shoot you both." He had his hand trembling next to his sidearm.

When Rocky fell to the ground, he fell on his injured hand, grinding desert dirt deep into the wounds on his face and his hand. He was whimpering as he got to his feet. "I'll kill her myself," he said. He jerked her to her feet and pushed her off toward the trees and away from the springs. As they walked into the trees, he started to pull his revolver when Chasing Rabbits whirled and smashed a big rock she had been concealing into his face.

She was fast on her feet and was through the trees and out into the desert dotted with brush and cedar. She hiked her buckskin skirts high and was running as fast as her long four-teen-year-old legs would carry her and found a deep arroyo. Chasing Rabbits dropped into it, got under a big sage along its side, and almost buried herself. Rocky and Curly Joe did not attempt to find the girl, Joe saying good riddance. Rocky wanted to track her down and kill her twice and Joe just laughed at him.

"She'll be dead in a day or two and we'll be in Boise drinking whiskey, Rocky. Wash your damn face, you look like a clown. We'll find a bank or two and get back into the business we know best, but you better not ever try to kidnap a woman again or I'll slice your manhood off and feed it to the dogs."

Rocky used water from the spring to try to clean the wound, Curly Joe refusing to help, and was alternating between howling oaths and screaming in pain. A great chunk of upper thumb meat was dangling, covered now in mud instead of just dirt, and Rocky finally just poured very hot water over the wound and wrapped it with some torn shirt tail.

Neither man heard one of the horses being led away during the night, never heard it being saddled and bridled, never heard it slowly walk back toward the main road and be put into a gentle lope as its rider made tracks for Burns, Oregon.

"Get up!" Curly Joe was screaming, kicking Rockefeller. "She stole your horse, you dumb sumbitch. Get up," and he kicked him again. Simpson was in a rage, trying to get his horse saddled, making so much noise and clamor that the horse was trying to shy off.

Rockefeller was slow to come out of his blanket, his hand swollen to twice its size from the bite and filth in the wound. "My horse? Gone? What are you talking about, Curly Joe, that's my horse you're saddling."

"Not anymore, it ain't." He kept right on trying to get the animal cinched. Rocky finally began to understand and, with a roar, rushed toward Curly Joe just as the outlaw stepped into the saddle. Curly Joe kicked Rockefeller square in the face as the man charged and turned the horse to gallop off.

Rockefeller lunged and grabbed a stirrup skirt and felt Simpson kick him again and again. The horse was fully spooked, rearing, kicking, whirling in a circle, kicking the morning fire and spreading hot coals into Rockefeller's bedroll. Curly Joe kept kicking Rockefeller in the head over and over until the big man finally let go and Curly Joe Simpson rode off to the northeast, cross-country.

Rockefeller rolled over in the desert dirt a couple of times before getting his feet under him, pulled his revolver and emptied it at the fleeing Simpson, never coming close at the extreme range. He walked over to the fire, grabbed his bedroll and tried to get the flames out. He got the campfire put back together and added some wood, made a pot of coffee, and cussed longer and louder than he ever had. His last thoughts were to clean the wounds but should have been his first.

It was at least a full half hour before the complete picture came to him, that he was alone, God knew how many miles from wherever, no horse, and no food. More than anything else, he thought of how many ways he could kill Curly Joe and Chasing Rabbits. The wounds to his face were bad enough but the bite Chasing Rabbits put on Rockefeller's hand could quickly lead to the man's death.

He knew he was in more trouble than he had ever been in his life but having little common sense, little basic knowledge of how to survive unless surrounded by others making wise decisions, Rockefeller simply sat down near the fire, drinking hot coffee and cussing at the top of his lungs.

CHAPTER TEN

"Whatcha got, tracker?" Buckmaster had his patrol halted near where Simpson and Rockefeller had turned north.

"Outlaws turned north at this point, Lieutenant," the Paiute tracker said. "Three men from the Lazy U Ranch also turned and are following the outlaws. They are many hours ahead of us, I think."

"Where does this road lead us?"

"Looks to be heading toward Burns in Grant County, Oregon. I'm sure these men are not really going there."

"Why do you say that?" Lieutenant Buckmaster wanted to press the chase and also wanted to hear what the tracker had to offer.

"Shaggy Hair's father is sheriff in Grant County. They not go there." Crazy Dog was Dancing Antelope's nephew and was chuckling thinking what would happen if the two outlaws ended up in Sheriff Schultz's custody. "Shaggy Hair plenty angry."

"Let's follow then," Buckmaster said. It had taken far too long to organize the troop for the chase, men spread all around the village, and then to find a tracker who knew the area. The thought came to him again. Why are we always following and not really chasing these bad guys and Indian raiders? "Stay on their trail, Crazy Dog, and pick up the pace if you can." He stood tall in the stirrups, raised his arm and gave the command, "Forward, ho."

They ran out of daylight and found a convenient place to camp. "We'll get an early start, Sergeant. Have your men ready to ride well before dawn." More than frustrating knowing that any one of those troopers could put in eighteen hours or more in the saddle yet were camped at sundown. It came to him a bit later that, since he was in command, it should have been his decision not the sergeant's. His first real command wasn't starting out well. This wasn't what he had learned at the Academy and the reason it wasn't working was he'd always followed orders. Listen, Lieutenant Buckmaster, sir, the only one on this patrol who is giving orders is me. He wanted to chuckle through his anger at his own lack of experience.

"Whatever created that dust storm ended and it looks like someone rode off," Brownie said.

They were riding toward the stand of trees at a brisk trot and spotted Rockefeller sitting with his back to them at the fire. He was so busy cussing, trying to clean his wounds, and thinking of ways to kill, he never heard the group slowly walk into camp.

"Hello, Rocky Feller. You fall off your horse again?" Dancing Antelope jumped off his horse and whacked the big outlaw across the side of head with his rifle butt. "Where's Chasing Rabbits? Where?" He had the rifle up to his shoulder, aimed straight into the big man's mouth.

"Easy does it, Dancing Antelope," Corcoran said, walking up beside the Paiute. "Let's not kill him yet. He's got a long story to tell us." Dancing Antelope slowly lowered the rifle but never let the aim change.

"This big mess, Corcoran." Dancing Antelope was chuckling as he looked around the camp. "Seems you lose your horse, Rocky Feller. Betcha Chasing Rabbits has it. That was those other prints we saw, Corcoran. She is the fastest Paiute in the world. She don't need a horse, Rocky Feller, but she took yours because she don't like you." He let the rifle come all the way down and stood back with an ugly grin on his face. "You die soon, I think."

"I think you're right. That was Curly Joe we saw riding out but there was just the one horse. Dancing Antelope, ride back to the main road and follow that trail. Chasing Rabbits is running for Burns and Shaggy Hair's father. Go, and ride hard."

The Paiute was on his horse and at a full gallop instantly. "Brownie, we have us a little problem. What are we gonna do with this yahoo? I want to chase down Curly Joe and I want to keep this man in custody and we have but two horses. Any good thoughts?"

"There's only one way to make this work. One of us rides hard after Simpson and the other brings Rockefeller to Burns. The good part of this, Corcoran, they have given up their rights to the homestead." Both men laughed and Brownie took the opportunity to poke Rockefeller hard in the ribs with his rifle then mock him as Dancing Antelope would.

"You're not laughing, Rocky Feller," he joshed. "I'll get after Curly Joe and you tend to this fool. It's about a ten-mile walk. He'll make it."

The two men shook hands and Brownie was in the saddle and on his way across the vast plain of the Nevada-Oregon borderland. "First beer's on you when this is over, Brownie," Corcoran hollered, watching Brownie give his horse a gentle nudge with his spurs.

"So, Mr. Rockefeller, it seems it's just us on the trail again," Corcoran snickered. "Gather what you want from this pigsty of a camp and let's get moving. A nice ten-mile hike on a beautiful fall morning should make you feel much better.

"The thing is, you see, I really do want to kill you. You ruined the lives of Nate and Susan Coppersmith, you abducted and God knows what you did to Chasing Rabbits, and you physically attacked a lady I have a lot of good feelings about. Yes sir, Rocky Feller, I do want to kill you. Now, git to walking and if you do slack, I'll shoot you down like the filthy dog you are."

Corcoran took every opportunity to get answers about what Simpson was really after as far as Coppersmith's ranch was concerned. "What brought all that on, Rocky?" he asked. "What made you and Simpson take over the ranch?"

"Don't know," Rocky said. "Something in a letter he got when we were in Arizona. Me and Slant Eyed Tom rode north to Nevada, to Austin, to rob the bank there and Simpson told us to meet him at this ranch. We were supposed to run the ranch for a short time and then sell it, then he changed his mind, and then changed his mind again."

No matter how many times Corcoran asked, it became clear that Rockefeller had no idea what might have been in that letter or who it might have come from. His first thoughts were Sheriff Peters but he also wondered about Reginald Chapman, the land agent.

"Do you know Reg Chapman or Pete Peters?" He didn't follow through with the titles.

"I've heard the names but don't know 'em. Seems like Simpson talked about someone named Chapman, but don't remember."

After a time, Corcoran just got quiet and let the man walk on toward Burns. Sure would be nice to know what was in that letter and who it was from. Gotta be Peters or Chapman but all his thoughts didn't mean digger dog without that letter.

"Betsy," David Schultz stammered. He had heard pounding on his cabin door just about sunset and found his daughter, bruised face and all, trying to get in. "What on earth? My God, girl, what happened to you?" He got her in the house and seated at the kitchen table. "Whoever did this to you is a dead man," he said, softly, dangerously. He poured them each a cup of coffee and laced both with some good bourbon.

"Take your time, girl, because I want to know everything. Somebody is going to die." After Betsy's mother was killed in a Bannock raid many years ago, David Schultz had dedicated his life to giving Betsy the best and safest life he could. One of the main reasons he became a lawman.

Betsy knew full well that she was a woman, an attractive woman, but was raised to be tough, to be self-protective, and on the frontier, to not take crap from anyone. She drank her whiskey straight, told ribald stories with a wry sense of humor, and flirted with men at every opportunity. At the same time, when the situation called for it, she was the lady from the East Coast who would never get her pinkies the least bit dirty.

He brought a bowl of warm water and some toweling to the table so she could clean up some, and filled two bowls with lamb stew he had simmering on the cast iron wood stove.

"Wash your face, eat something hearty, and tell me what happened." He stood next to her chair, his big ham of a hand resting on her shoulder, and bent down to kiss the top of her unruly head of hair.

Betsy had the mind of a teacher and took her time as she told the story to her father of how Coppersmith lost his ranch

- he of course knew that part of the story - and how Simpson came to the village to sell the ranch. She went into great detail about the attack by Rockefeller, about the shooting of the trooper, and about the abduction of Chasing Rabbits.

The coffee pot and the stew pot were empty by the time she finished with the telling. "You need a good night's rest, my little heroine. But tomorrow there will be no rest as you and I go on the trail to find those bastards."

Betsy had seen her father angry more than once but when his voice got so very soft and his eyes got flinty black, she knew more than one person would die. "They left town as if they were going back to the ranch, Papa. Dancing Antelope was right on their trail."

"Then that's where we'll start. We'll light out about dawn and ride toward the Sleepy U. Brown and Corcoran along with Dancing Antelope will all be there. Those men will die for what they've done."

Breakfast was done with and horses were saddled just as the sun peeked its head above the horizon. They had bedrolls and enough food to get them a good lunch on the ride to the ranch, and rode out at a strong trot, eating up miles of Nevada-Oregon desert.

About five miles out of town they saw a horse off in the sagebrush with a rider slumped in the saddle and rode quickly over. "It's Chasing Rabbits," Betsy hollered, picking up the reins to the slowly walking horse.

They got the girl off the horse and on a bedroll, gave her a drink of water, and waited for an answer to the hundreds of questions they had. Her face was bloody and bruised, and she was sore from so many times Rockefeller had hit her. She was hungry as she hadn't eaten for at least twenty-four hours nor had she slept except for the last hour in the saddle when she couldn't stay awake any longer.

Schultz got a fire started and a pot of coffee made while Betsy held the sobbing teenager. "At least they didn't ... you know ...," she let her voice trail off and Schultz nodded. Betsy held her as tight as Chasing Rabbits held her and they sat in the dust and dirt, rocking back and forth.

Schultz put a couple of chunks of jerky in a cup of hot coffee for the girl and when it softened, she ate it like a wolf on a lamb. Some hot food and a good face washing and the girl was ready for the day. Chasing Rabbits said she was okay and wanted to ride with them. "You ketch big moose and beat him, Shaggy Hair."

"I will," Betsy said and David Schultz had it in his mind that she probably would do just that.

They finished the pot of coffee, Chasing Rabbits ate half a pound of cornbread and some more chunks of smoked bear meat, then they started their ride to the Sleepy U. They made about another five miles and found another rider coming toward them at a fast trot.

"That's Dancing Antelope," Betsy said. Chasing Rabbits squealed her delight at seeing her uncle and Schultz wondered who else might be on this trail.

"Got big story to tell, Sheriff," Dancing Antelope said. "Almost catched those fellers, we did. Make coffee," he said. "We talk."

Another fire was lit and another pot of coffee was brewed. The four had their horses tied off on some nearby cedar bushes and they sat in the dirt around a warming fire, listening to Dancing Antelope tell his story about trailing Simpson and Rockefeller, and him coming to Burns to find

Chasing Rabbits and to get the sheriff. "Guess my job all done." Dancing Antelope chuckled.

"Just starting," Schultz almost snarled. "So Simpson is heading northeast, eh?" He sat very quiet for a few minutes and finally seemed to reach some kind of conclusion. "Okay, then. Here's what we have to do. Betsy, you take Chasing Rabbits back to my house. Dancing Antelope, you ride with me and we'll follow Corcoran and Brownie.

"We'll have those bastards in chains or hanging from a cottonwood before supper. Let's get it on," he said standing quickly.

"No, no, no," Betsy said. "No, no. I'm not riding back to Burns and neither is Chasing Rabbits. No, Papa. We're a big part of this. We're the ones all beat up and bruised. We're the ones looking for blood, Papa. We're going with you." The set of her jaw and strength of her voice was something Schultz had heard and seen more than once and he knew the argument was over.

She stood with her legs spread just a bit, as a gunman might; her shoulders were squared and her jaw was set. Betsy's eyes sparkled in defiance and Schultz noticed even her fists were balled and ready.

David Schultz had had fights like this with his daughter so many times over the years

and knew that no matter how strong his argument was, hers was the one that would win.

Dancing Antelope, though, wanted the two women on the ride. "Sure, Shaggy Hair, you come with us and bring Chasing Rabbits. We go now, catch 'em bad mens."

Schultz simply said, "Okay, fine," and they mounted up and headed toward Simpson's last camp.

"Damnedest posse I've ever rode with," Schultz muttered watching his daughter and the two Indians trot off in front of him. "Probably gonna be the best one, too." He had to laugh and at the same time had another worry come to mind. Chasing Rabbits had already eaten the only food they'd brought with them on what was supposed to be a quick ride to the Sleepy U ranch. He needed to talk to Dancing Antelope about that.

"We don't have much grub with us, Dancing Antelope. We were headed for the ranch. You and Corcoran have food?"

"Yeah, we took food from Sleepy U kitchen but not much. We catch or kill food, Sheriff Man. No problem."

CHAPTER ELEVEN

"Sergeant Banion, I want to move hard and fast today. We've lost a lot of time, moved too slow, and I want those outlaws under restraints as soon as possible." Lieutenant Buckmaster had finally put himself in command of the operation where he should have been at some point the day before.

"Yes sir," Banion said. He turned to the troopers who were putting their gear together. "We're moving out in five. Let's move it, boys. That little girl is depending on us."

"Hell, just an injun kid. Who cares?" one trooper was heard to say.

"I care," Buckmaster said and stormed over to the trooper. "Stand at attention when I talk to you, soldier. Put this man on report, Sergeant Banion. The United States Army is responsible for these Paiute and Shoshone people and, by damn, we will protect them and try to keep them safe. That little girl was abducted by known criminals and it is our responsibility to see to it that she is saved. The next man to speak as this one did will be held for criminal intent. Mount up, we're moving out."

Buckmaster rode at the front of the patrol with Lazy Dog

doing the tracking. He had just the slightest grin on his face as he put his horse in a strong lope. By damn, I like this concept of command. He kept the patrol in a lope for half an hour, brought them down to a walk for half an hour, then back to a lope again.

"We have riders in front of us, sir," the tracker said, pointing at some dust off a mile or so. "Too far away to make 'em out."

"Be aware, but ride out and see who they are," Buckmaster said. "We'll slow to a walk until you return."

He watched the big Paiute ride off and brought the troop to a walk. It looked like four or five horses but he couldn't tell for sure. Finally, he reined up and pulled his telescope out. "Four riders, Banion. Looks like two women and two men. At least one of the men is an Indian. Probably not connected with who we're chasing. Let's ride."

The two groups came together at the point where Simpson and Rockefeller had turned more toward the east. It was not a long pow-wow as Schultz and Betsy outlined what had transpired. "So this Deputy Brown and Corcoran are chasing Simpson now?" Buckmaster was on his haunches along with Schultz, Dancing Antelope, and Sergeant Banion.

"Well, you folks can go on home then. The army will take over the chase and bring that man to justice."

"I don't think so, Lieutenant," Schultz said. "I'm the sheriff of this county and that's a wanted man that Corcoran and Brown are chasing. He's mine and I'll be part of bringing him in." Schultz had been through this so many times over the years that it didn't really rile him like it used to. He was almost chuckling remembering he just had this discussion about jurisdictional problems with Deputy Brown.

"He shot and killed one of my troopers, Sheriff. He's a federal fugitive. He's mine and the army will bring him in."

The two men were sitting on their haunches in the

Oregon dirt, staring at each other, both determined to bring Simpson to justice. From Schultz's point of view, of course, he was right; from Buckmaster's, of course, he was. Usually in a dispute such as this, the army wins but Schultz was bound and determined to not be left out of the chase and capture. It was his daughter who was attacked and beaten.

Dancing Antelope squared himself some and said, "White mans make a mess of even simple job. I ride now to find Corcoran and Brown Man and finish job. Chasing Rabbits, you ride with me."

"I'm riding with you, too, Dancing Antelope," Betsy said.

"Good. Shaggy Hair need to punch man in face."

"You're all crazy," David Schultz said, "and I guess you might include me in that. Let's mount up. We're wasting time talking. You do as you please, Lieutenant, we're chasing Curly Joe Simpson."

"That's right," Dancing Antelope said. "When we catch big fool, we divide him so army get their share." He was ready to put heels to his horse. The others would fall in with him and Buckmaster and Banion would eat some dust.

"Hold on there," Buckmaster said. "Let's work this out without the animosity. Sheriff Schultz, I can understand your claim to the outlaw and I hope you can see mine. Dancing Antelope might have a point. Let's work together. I'm sure you'll move faster than we will; just make sure you're on the right trail."

Schultz swallowed a bit of his pride as did the young lieutenant. They shook hands and it was Dancing Antelope that gave the command, "Let's ride," laughing as he did, getting a prod and chuckle from Shaggy Hair.

They made about two miles when Dancing Antelope spotted Corcoran and Rockefeller coming toward them. "This is turning into a full circus out here." Schultz chuckled. "Good to see you, Corcoran, and the prisoner you've got in hand."

Chasing Rabbits cowered at the sight of Rockefeller and Betsy moved her horse in between quickly. She didn't want to but she edged the two of them away from the rest of the group; she wanted to ride up alongside Corcoran and stay right there. "It's alright," she whispered to Chasing Rabbits. "He can't hurt you. I know we both have been hurt by him but he can't hurt us again." She carried a Bowie knife on her belt and gave it a good pat as she nodded to the frightened girl.

"Well, we're in a pickle now," Schultz said. "What do we do with this fool?"

"Hang him," Dancing Antelope said.

"No trees," Corcoran laughed. "I been looking for one."

"You keep right on walking him down the trail. There's an army patrol coming our way. You can turn your prisoner over to Lieutenant Buckmaster and then ride back and join us. We're moving out to catch up with Brownie. Let's get it on," he said, stepping into the stirrup.

"Hold up just a minutes, Schultz," Corcoran said. "Old Rocky Feller here tells me that Simpson got some kind of letter from someone that caused him to come north and work to take over Coppersmith's Sleepy U ranch. Have any of you heard anything about that?" He looked around the group, getting just shakes of their heads.

"That letter might be what started this fracas and would certainly indicate a conspiracy somewhere. Did he get a letter from Sheriff Peters? From the land agent? Whatever, at least now we can get word to Coppersmith that Simpson has vacated his homestead and he can reclaim it." Corcoran prodded Rockefeller and walked off down the trail toward the army patrol.

An hour later, Corcoran rode up to the group with Lieutenant Buckmaster alongside. "With a wounded prisoner in hand, I sent Sergeant Banion back with the patrol. That man's hand needs to be looked at. I'll ride with you, Sheriff Schultz."

"You're welcome, of course, Buckmaster. Just keep in mind it's my posse. With

Dancing Antelope along, we will ride Simpson down soon. He's never lost a man or a steer, I believe."

There had been so much activity that Schultz didn't even think about rations and cussed himself a couple of hours later when he realized he could have gotten some from the army.

They rode for the rest of the day, spread out along the trail left by Brownie and Simpson. It was easy to follow. Chasing Rabbits didn't like riding horses and spent most of her time running or walking alongside Betsy. They were friends from years back and were now sisters in trouble, if you will. There was a lot of talk, laughter, even a couple of old Paiute songs.

"Let's nest up over in those trees," Schultz said as the sun began its final descent and the air offered a serious chill. "Get a good fire going, Betsy. Dancing Antelope, Buckmaster, we need to talk for a couple of minutes."

The three men walked along the trail, back and forth, as David Schultz pointed out several times that they had no food with them. Dancing Antelope seemed to just pass it off as if that meant little or nothing to him.

"Don't you understand? We're off in the desert, miles from nowhere, with two women and no food. We're in trouble."

"Not in trouble, sheriff man. You'll see. Come sit by fire. We filled canteens at spring, no problem."

Buckmaster said that he had some supplies in his saddlebags but not very much. "When we left," Schultz said, "we were riding toward the Sleepy U ranch, less than a day's ride, and knew there would be food at the ranch. None of all this," and he waved his hands about, "was in our thoughts."

Shultz just shook his head, knew he had no other choice, and sat by the fire with Betsy and Dancing Antelope. "Where's Chasing Rabbits?"

"She be back soon, sheriff man. Ah, here comes Corcoran. Hey, you gots food in saddlebags?"

Corcoran just nodded and sat down. Buckmaster was with him. He looked around the group, gave Betsy a big smile. "Where's your little companion?"

"I haven't seen her for an hour or more, Terrence. She said she'd be right back but I'm starting to worry."

"No worry, Shaggy Hair," Dancing Antelope said.

"That was some flowery language you used when I dropped Rockefeller in your lap, Lieutenant." Corcoran chuckled, throwing more wood on their fire. "They teach you to cuss like that at the Academy?"

Buckmaster chuckled, reddened a bit remembering some of the things he'd said, and picked up a short stick to ponder on some. He glanced at Betsy and found she was looking him in the eye as well. The redness returned and he concentrated on that stick in his hand.

Corcoran wouldn't let it go, though. He was having just a bit of fun at making the soldier a bit uncomfortable. "Buckmaster said that when we caught Curly Joe we had best remember that he is a federal fugitive, also. There were threats involved in what he said." The laughter could have been heard for some distance if anyone was out and about.

"We still have this big problem of food, or more like it, no food," Schultz said. He was more than perplexed that no one seemed to care whether they survived this desert ordeal.

His timing was perfect as Chasing Rabbits came into the camp carrying two big hares. "Ah, Chasing Rabbits, you did good," Dancing Antelope said. "Dinner, Mr. Sheriff Man," he chortled.

Chasing Rabbits had the animals dressed and ready for the fire in minutes and Corcoran produced coffee and some hard biscuits from his saddlebags. Supper consisted of roasted rabbit and wild onions along with some good chatter.

"Is that where you got your name?" Terrence Corcoran was more than impressed with what he'd seen. "You chased those big hares down?"

"Sure she did," Dancing Antelope said. "Fastest runner in whole world, Corcoran. "She can't catch antelope, gotta shoot them critters or trap 'em, but anything else you want caught, Chasing Rabbits will catch 'em up good."

Chasing Rabbits was sitting as close to Betsy as she could get, her head down, looking into the fire. Betsy put her arm around the girl and whispered something to her. Chasing Rabbits looked up and smiled. "Yes, Shaggy Hair, I can run as fast as horse sometimes."

"You've got one fine posse, Sheriff," Buckmaster said. "All we have to do now is catch up with your deputy and take Curly Joe into custody."

"Sure wish it would be that simple, Lieutenant. I don't suppose you have a flask in those saddlebags?"

"Yup," is all the man said. The fire was warm and the group sat around it, the flask moving back and forth among the white men. Dancing Antelope had tried whiskey once and vowed he would never try it again, and Betsy and Chasing Rabbits wouldn't have been offered any anyway. At her home was one thing; in public, in front of men, no.

"I would sure feel better if you women rode back to the village," Buckmaster said. "This is just no place for a lady to be. The dangers on a chase like this are more than a woman can face."

"That isn't going to happen, Lieutenant," Betsy said. Her

voice was strong, that of a schoolteacher and frontier woman. "I was born and raised on the frontier, sir, and this chase isn't anymore dangerous than a ride through the desert. I've got a Paiute brave, a sheriff, another lawman, and an army man for protection."

She tried to smile through her anger. "Besides that, sir. My mama died fighting right next to my papa. I've fought next to him, too. You're from the East Coast and the ladies there might not be able to withstand the rigors of the frontier but I know for a fact that you wouldn't have had supper tonight if it weren't for Chasing Rabbits, and I'll stand next to my papa and fight Curly Joe Simpson to the death if need be.

"He's a butcher, a mad killer, and he's robbed the livelihood from a good friend of mine. No, sir, Lieutenant, I'm riding with this posse."

A red-faced and chagrined Lieutenant Roland Buckmaster walked to his bedroll and called it a night. Prettiest girl I think I've ever met, he thought, and sure as I'm born, the most one way.

Betsy's thoughts as she wrapped up in her bedroll were on Terrence Corcoran; those wonderful eyes and his long flowing reddish curls. *I'll fight alongside you, Corcoran, any time, any place.* Corcoran was walking around the campsite, stopped at the fire and added a couple of chunks of wood, then stopped next to Betsy.

"You sleep well, lovely lady. I'm sure glad you're on our side." He gave her a big smile and walked some more around the camp.

CHAPTER TWELVE

"I'm going to have it out with that fool, Susan," Nate Copper-smith said. He, his wife, and Seamus Doherty were in the Coppersmith's cabin's kitchen discussing what took place at the saloon earlier. Coppersmith was still seething with anger. "My ranch, my cattle, my life stolen, and the man with the badge laughs in my face."

"It might sound wrong to say this, Nate, but you've got to let those of us fighting for you do our part. Peters will get his, I'll see to that and welcome your help at the time. But this isn't the time." Doherty was actually pleading with the man, knowing that anything he might do would put Coppersmith in jail and jeopardize what Corcoran was trying to do.

"We both have thoughts that somewhere along the line there is a conspiracy of some kind to put Curly Joe Simpson at your ranch and then take it over. To create another problem by attacking the sheriff or that ass Chapman will affect our investigation. Between that big Irisher and this one," he chuckled, jerking a thumb toward himself, "you'll have your ranch back and soon." Doherty was back in the saddle, a detective for Wells Fargo for so many years and he was working again.

"Listen to him, Nate. We all want this to end but we want it to end right, not with you in jail or worse. Please." Susan was crying and had been since Nate told her of the meeting he had with Peters in the saloon.

"It was an open challenge, Susan. He dared me, mocked me, and I wanted to shoot that bastard...oh, I'm so sorry for my language." He found no words and just sat, quaking in anger, and looked from one to the other.

"I'm going to have another talk with Peters," Seamus said. "He can't go on acting this way despite his anger at you. I'll force him to accept his responsibility as sheriff of this county. For me to do that, I'm acting as a concerned citizen, but for you to do that puts you and what we're working on in jeopardy."

It was a short walk across the tracks and to the Humboldt County Courthouse for a visit with Pete Peters and Doherty took that time to try to put together an argument that would stimulate the man into action. "I'm afraid our sheriff is carrying so much anger it's poisoned his ability to reason, to understand what Simpson has done."

He was back being a lawman. No matter what he said to this man or to Chapman, he must keep in mind that possibility of a conspiracy and which of the two might be involved. Neither one could know his suspicions.

Seamus walked into the sheriff's office without a clue of what to say to the man, except, "Pete, we need to talk like reasonable men."

"Don't talk to me about reasonable. I've got much bigger problems right now. Get out of my way," he snarled, almost running from his office, carrying a shotgun in one hand and a rifle in the other.

Seamus watched him join with four other armed men, all

deputies, gathered on the street. They mounted and rode at a fast trot on the road north toward Fort McDermott. Doherty stood in the office and looked at the jailer. "What's going on, Ramon?"

"Pete got a message from Fort McDermott. Something about a trooper being shot."

"Looks like the sheriff will actually have to do his job," Seamus said, shaking his head as he walked out of the big building. "Well, at least Nate won't be going after him if he's out of town."

He took that moment to quickly glance over Peters' desk and saw the poster detailing Simpson's little gang and the rewards being offered. Murder, bank robbery, kidnapping were the highlighted crimes, and a figure of $5,000 was offered for their capture or death.

It's on top of all the broadsheets and he's been sitting there staring at that poster. He's either having second thoughts and is going after Simpson or he's a part of the problem and is wondering how to keep it from getting bigger. I need to talk to Chapman again.

It was a long ride from Winnemucca to Fort McDermott which was located on the far northern Nevada border with Oregon. The message had come from his deputy, Aural Douglas, and Captain Wayne Watson, the McDermott commanding officer. Peters re-read that message in his head, over and over.

It said in plain English that Curly Joe Simpson - wanted for murder, bank robbery, and other crimes, and a known resident of Humboldt County - had shot and killed a soldier attached to Fort McDermott, at a small Indian village west of the fort. The note didn't ask the question directly but Peters knew that Captain Watson would. Why, the captain would demand, hadn't Simpson been arrested as soon as the wanted broadsheets arrived?

It was a long two-day ride north with the four deputies, each asking about what they were doing and Peters being as vague as he possibly could. At camp the first night, Chief Deputy Sam Messing got Peters aside and put it plainly. "Don't rightly know what it is we're doing, Sheriff, but I do believe it's time you told us. Are we riding into a fight with the army, with Indians, or what? We have a right to know."

"It's probably gonna be all cleared up by the time we get there. A soldier got shot by a civilian in the village west of the fort. The army thinks it's our job to catch the man. Douglas will probably have him in custody by the time we get there."

"Is it one of our fine outlaw citizens or from out of the county? You must have some information." Messing was not normally a questioning type of deputy but the way the sheriff was trying to hide whatever information he had bothered him. "You're holding something from us, Sheriff, and I really don't think that's right."

"I'm the sheriff, you're chief deputy, and we're riding to catch a killer. That's all you need to know." Peters limped back to the fire and poured a cup of coffee, not looking at any of the men. He thought: I'm gonna be forced to face this and it's all Nate Coppersmith's fault. I wouldn't be sheriff if he hadn't got me all stove up, and he wouldn't have lost his ranch if he hadn't had a sickly kid. I ought to just keep riding and let Messing handle it. Give him my badge and ride on north to wherever.

The idea of simply riding off kept him awake for many hours that night and the more he thought about it, the more he wanted to do just that. *I can't ride for a brand again, not with my bad legs, and I'll probably never wear a badge again. But if I just ride off, I got enough savvy about life that I'll survive just fine.*

Peters and the deputies rode into Fort McDermott about

three in the afternoon accompanied by winds blowing at least forty miles per hour and a storm building to unleash the rest of its fury a bit later. They rode to the resident deputy's residence instead of the fort commander's office. Protocol would have suggested a visit to the Post Commander first.

"Any news from the army?" Peters spat the question without even saying hello to the man. "I suppose Watson wants to see me."

"He does, indeed, Sheriff, and he's one angry sumbitch. Hope you got some good answers for him."

"Mind your words, Douglas. You and the men stay here. I'll go see Watson."

"No, Sheriff, Captain Watson wants you, Chief Deputy Messing, and me to meet with him as soon as you got here. He saw you ride in, I'm sure, so we'd best get over there."

"Just who do you work for, Douglas? Me or the army?"

"I'm a guest on their fort, Sheriff. It was Humboldt County that approved this idea of having a resident deputy at the fort, but I am a guest and have to remember that all the time. It's not a good idea to get the commanding officer riled."

The procession to the commander's office was led by Aural Douglas, not the sheriff, Captain Watson noted, watching them out his window. Certainly not the way he would do it. His thoughts at all times were simply this: Leaders lead. Nothing else matters. He stuck his head out of the office and told his orderly to have the sheriff and his party wait for a few.

"I'll tell you when to bring them in." There was a decided snicker as he said that and the orderly did what he could to hide his smile knowing what a sadistic bastard the captain was and enjoying his part in the drama. After a long fifteen minutes, Captain Wayne Watson ushered the gentlemen into his office. There were no seating accommodations.

Watson walked behind his simple wooden desk and sat. "I hope you have some explanation for this," he said, offering a copy of the wanted poster with Curly Joe, Rocky, and the dead Slant Eyed Tom featured in full face. "I'm sure you've seen a copy of this."

Peters stood, silent, but Sam Messing strode forward to look at the poster. "Those are the men that worked for Nate Coppersmith. You helped that Simpson feller get possession of that ranch." He spun on the sheriff, glaring at him. "Say something, dammit."

"I don't remember seeing that poster," Peters said. "What was it this Simpson did, Captain?"

"You are a worthless piece of hog shit, mister," Captain Watson snarled. "If it were in my power, I'd rip that badge off your coat and ram it up your arse. Every law office in the western states and territories is in receipt of these broadsheets so you are also a scum-covered liar," he bellowed loud enough to scare the hell out of a couple of privates walking by outside.

"This man Simpson murdered one of my troopers," he said. "Simpson's been living the good life in your county for almost a year. He and the vile rapist Rockefeller attacked a white woman and kidnapped an Indian girl," the captain raged, jumping from his seat and thrusting his head across the desk, forcing Peters to take a step back.

"What are you going to do about this, Sheriff?" Watson said that almost softly as he sat back down. He reached in his desk for a cigar and took his time getting it lit. He bit the end off and spat it halfway across the room. Fumbled about for a light, finally getting the cigar lit. He took a long draw and blew the smoke toward the ceiling. "Tell me your plans, sir."

Peters stood mute, quaking at the outburst, looking out the window at some soldiers drilling on the parade grounds, a million thoughts flying through his muddled mind, not one of which would satisfy the captain. Captain Watson sat quietly, drumming his fingers on the desktop, taking a puff or two on his cigar. A slow smile, evil and intense, spread across the CO's face.

Aural Douglas knew better than to say anything and Sam Messing was just as angry at the sheriff as Watson so he wouldn't say anything either. The silence continued for at least one full minute before Watson slammed his hand onto the desktop one more time. "Orderly!"

The corporal rushed into the office almost knocking Messing aside. "Take that man's weapon and escort him to the guardhouse." He turned to Sheriff Peters, a scowl so embedded it might never go away. "Your malfeasance has cost the life of one of my troopers, Sheriff, and I'm holding you responsible for his death and the assault on a white woman and the kidnapping of an Indian girl.

"Get him out of here." The orderly grabbed Peters' sidearm with one hand and took a firm hold of an arm with the other, and marched him out of the office. Messing and Douglas stood quietly, not really sure what to do.

"Let's repair to your quarters, Mr. Douglas. We are about to have a long discussion on the responsibilities of a lawman." Captain Wayne Watson stood and escorted the deputies out of the office.

"The idea of becoming a man carries a heavy load that most of us are quite capable of handling," he said, almost marching with the deputies trying to keep up. "One of those loads is called responsibility and is the heaviest of all. Some boys are too weak to become real men and it's that responsibility load that signals their failure at manhood.

"You just saw a complete failure of a man. What happens now?" He asked the question as Deputy Aural Douglas opened the door to his quarters, ushering everyone in. "I'll tell you what happens now. Messing, you're the chief deputy so you are designated to take your people back to Winnemucca and inform the officials of what just took place here.

"Questions?" He looked about the room filled with civilians, each wearing the badge of Deputy Sheriff, Humboldt County. "Your sheriff is now in federal custody and will face federal charges and penalties."

Douglas stayed at the fort and Messing, now the leading lawman in Humboldt County, led his group back to the county seat. "Thank you for your hospitality, Captain Watson. I'm sorry for the loss of your trooper. I'm sure somewhere, there are answers to this situation but I can't for the life of me see them right now."

It was a long slow ride back to Winnemucca for Sam Messing and the others. Messing discussed what their options were, how they would have to visit that ranch and also have to have a talk with Coppersmith.

"Coppersmith has had his ranch stolen right out from under him," Messing said at their campfire the first night, "but we don't know if what happened was legal or not. Was Peters involved? Damn, boys, we're in a pickle." He made up his mind he would have a chat with Seamus Doherty, the former Wells Fargo detective.

"Where did that poster the captain had come from, Messing?" One of the deputies had taken a long look at the broadsheet when Watson showed it around. "Those men have been in the area for some time."

"I believe that when we get back to town we'll find copies of those posters somewhere in Peters' files. By the look on the sheriff's face and his complete silence, I'd say he knew those men were outlaws and did nothing about it."

"Shithead is what I call him," the deputy said.

CHAPTER THIRTEEN

"Looks like we might be in Idaho." Brownie murmured to himself as he looked out across the broad plain of the Jordan Valley. "Not sure where Simpson wants to end up but he's working his way toward a couple of mining districts. The Jordan Valley has some fine ranches as well. I think he's off course."

Grant County Deputy Brown was sure that Simpson was going to try for Boise but he'd been veering more and more to the north. "The man's an outlaw and outlaws look for easy marks. Ranches ain't easy marks. Banks are. Gold shipments are. Express boxes, train cars. Time to put the press on this man and quit our riding around in the desert," he chuckled giving his horse a little nudge. "We're close enough to him that we could box him in somewhere tomorrow."

There was a frustration level kicking in brought about by being alone on the chase, not knowing very much about who was being chased, and always the fear of an ambush. Setting up an ambush in the open desert of the great basin wouldn't be difficult and Brownie didn't know if Simpson even knew he was being followed.

He made a good camp that night under some cottonwood trees with a small stream pouring out of a spring for water. There was plenty of grass to graze and Brownie had the remains of a sage grouse he'd shot the day before. "I bet that pretty white shirt Simpson was wearin' is all messed up now. I'm gonna catch up with him tomorrow."

It was an hour before light and Brown was on the trail. "There," he said, seeing just a wisp of smoke about half a mile ahead. "I knew I was close." He put his horse in a gentle lope until he got close and then brought the big horse to a walk. He got off and tied the horse to some cedar bushes and slowly made his way toward the smoke.

He could smell smoke from green wood, could smell coffee boiling, and maybe even some sidemeat frying as he slowly made his way through cottonwood deadfall. He was on his belly, looking through broken branches into an empty camp. Is he off doing his business? Getting wood? His blanket's are gone. He could see matted grass where Simpson had slept that night.

"Only one way to do this," he muttered, jumped to his feet, pulled his Colt, and rushed the camp. It was deserted but the coffee pot and tin cup were left behind. "Simpson must have heard me and ran like the dirty dog he is. Sumbitch," he said, "the man might go in any direction now."

He poured a cup since it was there, walked around the perimeter of the camp, and found where Simpson had his horse tethered, then found the track leading out. "Man's gonna ride into the sun this time," he said. "Boise has to be his destination and I'm just minutes behind him." He stopped and ate the sidemeat that was almost burnt crisp before getting back in the saddle. "Thankee," he snickered, wiping what little grease there was from his chin.

It was a typical fall day with bright warm sunshine, not much wind, and easy riding. Following Simpson's trail was a piece of cake. "That man knows I'm right behind him and he's not trying to hide anything. He'll never outrun this little pony."

He rode hard on the fresh track and saw a rocky hillside coming up in front. "If that doesn't say danger, I'll be danged. Simpson must be planning a little surprise party for this old boy." He had the horse at a walk and gave the hillside a full look-see. He could see a hundred spots for an ambush, could see two passes through the ridge, and calculated as best he could what Simpson might try. "I can hide you down in that dry wash and let you graze some," he said to his horse. "I'm wasting a lot of time if he just rode through one of those passes but, if he's looking for a fight, he's gonna get one."

He tied the horse to some scrub brush in the wash with grass around it. He grabbed his Winchester and climbed out of the wash. Brownie crab-walked through heavy brush and got down behind some rocks where he could hunker down with his long-glass and not be seen by anyone on the rocky hillside. "I think old Curly Joe was headed for that pass on the right," he mumbled and started sweeping the rocks with the glass.

This was rough country with the vast Jordan Valley to the north and still many miles from the Snake River and Boise country. It looked like some giants got angry at the mountains and just ripped them up and threw them back down. The rocks were tumbled against each other, broken and scarred, scattered about like discarded junk. That pile of rock was stretched out for miles, north and south. "More than ten million places for a man to hide."

In less than half an hour, he had Curly Joe spotted. "Higher than I would have gone," he muttered. Curly Joe was standing alongside an outcrop looking out across the plain trying to find whoever it was following him. So far he hadn't spotted either Brownie or his horse. "Now, if I had a Henry

instead of this Winchester, I might try that shot." Brownie
chuckled knowing full well he wouldn't. "If I can get off to his
left and still be able to know where he is, I might be able to
get close tonight."

The tough deputy moved slowly from rock outcrop to
rock outcrop, from scrub cedar bush to scrub cedar bush, and
was well off to Simpson's left a couple of hours later. Simpson
hadn't moved from his perch but gave the impression of a
man getting nervous. "He hasn't seen me and he's wondering
if I've given up. It'd be a long cold shift in a deep mine before
I'd give up."

The sun was not a factor on this late fall afternoon but
the wind was. It started with little gusts and became a stiff
breeze that turned to near gale force. "We're gonna get wet
before long and cold, too," Brown muttered, watching dust
clouds billow through the valley below. There were high
clouds scudding through the ragged sky and black clouds
were building to the northwest as the day wore on.

"I think my best bet right now is either shoot this bad
man, capture him, or just give it all up. Number one or two
will be my options," he chuckled and started moving in for
the shot. "We need him alive and anywhere but Humboldt
County, Nevada so, Mr. Curly Joe, if I do have to shoot you,
I'll try not to kill you. That's gonna hurt, you know."

High winds were followed by driving rain and then the
temperature fell like a silver cartwheel at the saloon before
rain became ice and snow. Simpson wouldn't be one to sit in
vigil in a blizzard.

"I bet it snows hard tonight. I gotta get close enough to
take him before he rabbits on me. He'll give up the idea of an
ambush and light out. I wonder where he has his horse
tied off?"

Brownie used the weather to his advantage. The wind was
blowing clouds of dust and he moved when the dust

surrounded him. He was just above the base of the rocky hillside, found what was probably Simpson's prints leading into a
cleft in the rocks. Moving carefully, he slipped into the
opening and found Curly Joe's horse grazing peacefully and
out of the wind.

Simpson was in a hurry and simply tied the horse off.
Brownie finished the job by taking the saddle and bridle off
and hiding them in the brush. "Don't have to worry about
being quiet with this damn wind." He moved up higher into
the rocks, always making sure he knew where Simpson was.
He ducked behind a large outcrop and settled in, waiting for
the first opportunity to shoot the man.

Simpson got the first opportunity. Brownie spread himself
flat on the ground and took a look around the outcrop.
Simpson caught the movement and snapped off a quick shot
from his sidearm. Splinters of rock showered Brown as he
pulled back quickly. "Used his revolver. I wonder if that
means he doesn't have a rifle. My turn next, Curly Joe," he
chuckled.

"This was Brown Man's camp last night," Dancing Antelope
said, stirring the ashes in a small fire pit. "He not far in front
now. Storm coming, though." They had been fighting the
wind for several hours and knew they would be fighting rain
and snow before the day was over.

Corcoran and Dancing Antelope were usually in the lead
and Lieutenant Buckmaster was content to hold back and
ride next to Betsy as often as possible. Chasing Rabbits would
often foul his plans by running up alongside Betsy. Betsy
enjoyed the show and after a couple of hours let it go and
rode up front to be with Corcoran.

"How close do you think we are? With this wind, the
tracks get all messed up." She gave Corcoran a big smile.

When she turned back, she giggled seeing Chasing Rabbits running alongside Buckmaster's horse.

"Depending on how bad this storm's gonna be, I'd say we'll meet up with Brownie early in the morning. We're close but we're running out of daylight. You and that cute young cavalry officer making up?"

"If you mean Lieutenant Buckmaster, we have nothing to make up and I don't find him cute, Terrence. Actually, I find him rather attractive," she said. He humphed twice and wanted to spur Rube into a good hard trot but didn't.

"You sure were arguing pretty good this morning if I recollect. I guess it is, though, that a girl will be swayed by a uniform." All he got back was a "humph" as she turned her horse to rejoin Buckmaster. Corcoran laughed some as Schultz rode up; he thought, I like that kind of spunk in a woman but I'd like it better if she rode with me and not that soldier boy.

"Let's ride for another two hours at least and then camp up. From the looks of those clouds, we're gonna be wet and cold tonight." David Schultz got the troop moving a bit faster.

Chasing Rabbits grew tired of the games being played by Betsy and Buckmaster and ran off into the desert. Despite the high winds, dust being blown about in great clouds, she came running back in an hour later holding two large sage hens. "Good work," Corcoran said. He let the lithe girl swing up and ride awhile behind him.

"If we catch up with Brown Man today, it would be best. But that ain't gonna happen, Corcoran. This storm will wipe out any tracks we're following. Can't see through snow," Dancing Antelope said.

"Why don't you ride on ahead, Dancing Antelope. Leave good sign for us and try to catch up with Brownie. We won't be far behind you." Corcoran knew the big Paiute could ride fast and still read the trail. "Want one of these birds?"

"No. Got plenty food and coffee. I put marks on trees and bushes, Corcoran. You watch and see them," and he spurred his horse into a fast trot. He was out of sight in the dust in just moments.

"Shouldn't someone go with him? Two men would be better than one," Buckmaster said. He came up quickly after seeing Dancing Antelope ride off.

"Not in this case," Schultz said. "Word among the older Indians is that Dancing Antelope could track a wandering breeze if he felt like it. No, we'll ride strong, but he can ride hard and fast and give Brownie needed back-up before we get there. This storm is gonna make things difficult."

Tracking through grasses and dirt was one thing but doing it through rocks, gravel, and a frenzied blizzard was entirely different. A turned rock would not be noticed with snow blowing about and sticking to the ground. It was during bad winters that Indian trackers made their reputations, coming home with meat because they could. Dancing Antelope's family didn't fear winter hunger.

Corcoran found a copse of cottonwood trees and the barest of a spring and they set up camp. "Get a fair size fire ring built and we'll set out bedrolls and lean-tos as close as we dare." Great branches of broken cottonwood would burn all night and after the first were started, they raked coals off to the side and roasted the high-desert wild chickens.

"Chasing Rabbit's husband won't have much to do, I'm afraid," Corcoran laughed. "She'll provide as much food as he could eat." David Schultz noticed immediately that Corcoran had Betsy sitting on one side and Chasing Rabbits on the other. He also saw Lieutenant Buckmaster fidgeting some, wanting very much to move across the fire pit and sit much closer to Betsy.

This is turning out to be a much better chase than I expected. Schultz chuckled, wondering just how much fun Betsy was having. *She'll play that East Coast boy until he won't even know his own name and then run off with Corcoran.*

There was six to eight inches of icy snow to greet the group come morning but the wind had died to just a breeze. Fire, coffee, fried sidemeat were enjoyed in that order, and they were saddled and on the trail as the sky lightened for the coming day. Dancing Antelope had left good signs on sage brush, cedar brush, and whatever trees were available along Simpson's and Brown's trail.

"He must have ridden well into the night, Schultz," Corcoran said. "That man's amazing. Without his marks, we would have been wandering all over this desert. We'll be with him and Brownie in an hour or two I think." Even though they were riding through fresh snow, some drifts as deep as three feet, they found the going fairly good.

Simpson, while trying for Boise, was not following any known trail or road, was riding cross-country and had gotten off his aim for Boise and the Snake River. Without Dancing Antelope's markers, there was no trail in the snow to follow.

CHAPTER FOURTEEN

Dancing Antelope rode hard for the rest of the day and well into the twilight hours. He was about to give it up and make camp as the wind was blowing the snow so hard he couldn't see three feet in front of him, when he came to a deep ditch. "Looks like Brown Man rode into the ditch," he murmured and stepped off his horse. "Better be quiet so Brown Man don't shoot me."

He led the horse down into the arroyo and came nose to nose with Brownie's horse still

tied to a cedar bush. "Looks like I'll make camp right here," he chuckled, tying his horse off.

There was grass for the horse and plenty of scrub brush that Dancing Antelope could rip out of the ground for a fire. He used the sides of the gulch as a screen and was able to get a fair fire going after a few Paiute words that have never been successfully translated. Because of the raging storm, Dancing Antelope couldn't see the rocky hillside where Simpson was hiding.

It was not a pleasant night for any of them. Simpson had no protection from the weather other than what he was wearing and was in a rock formation a couple of hundred feet above where he thought whoever was following him was. "No fire, no blankets, no food. All because that fool Rocky smacked the woman and stole the Indian kid. I had to shoot the stupid soldier and now, just look."

Brownie was in a little better shape. He was nursing some rock dust cuts on his face and neck from the one shot that had been fired but they were minor. He walked back to Simpson's horse, found a bedroll on the saddle and some jerky in the saddlebags, and nested up for the night.

Dancing Antelope was the only one with a good fire and bedroll, and he ate well from the little kit Chasing Rabbits had fixed for him. He knew from the amount of snow falling that he would have trouble getting on Brownie's trail in the morning but didn't lose any sleep over it.

Dancing Antelope was nursing his fire into flames and heat as the sun made its appearance, and he saw the ragged hill where Simpson and Brown were. Stark white and towering into the heavens, it looked like a mass of rocks simply thrown about and covered in icing. The skies were clear and the wind had died to a gentle breeze. It was bitter cold but the sun would change that soon.

"Three passes that a man could use to get across that high hill," the big Paiute muttered, putting more wet sage on the fire. "The one on the right looks like the lowest pass but that one on the left looks like the easier one. Brown Man left his horse so he must know where the fool is."

Dancing Antelope drank two cups of hot coffee fast and climbed out of the deep gully. It wasn't hard to see where Brownie had climbed out, and it didn't take long to find just enough sign to give the man an idea of where Brown may have gone. When trying to follow someone who was also unfamiliar with the area, many trackers simply followed the terrain. It was what would be natural on the one hand and easiest on the other.

Dancing Antelope allowed the terrain to guide him into the rocks and he saw enough sign, disturbed rocks, broken limbs on brush, even a boot print or two where the wind wouldn't allow the snow to stick around. All this and he knew he was on the trail. His advance was slow and after about half an hour, he stopped suddenly. He couldn't see it but he could definitely smell smoke and boiling coffee.

"Good morning, Brown Man," he said with a smile. "Got enough coffee for two?"

"Well, well, well," Brownie laughed. "Look what the storm blew in. Anyone with you?" He put some more wood on the fire and found a second cup for Dancing Antelope.

"Be here later today. Looks like you fell down. Face all bloody."

"Simpson took a shot at me and hit some rocks. Just rock cuts. He's up along that line of rocks." He pointed up the hillside to a formation several hundred feet higher. "That's his horse over there so he ain't goin nowhere. There's a good little way up on the left there that puts me close enough for a good shot, but he didn't show himself much yesterday."

"Maybe you go up there and I go up on the other side and we put him in bear trap. Then we both shoot him. Twice," he laughed.

"We don't want to kill him, Dancing Antelope. It's okay to shoot the bastard," and he smiled and chuckled, "but we don't want to kill him. If that sheriff is part of this, or that land agent, we need to get that information. He has a rifle and his sidearm so let's be darned careful.

"You said they would be here later. Who and how many? I thought it was just you, me, and Corcoran."

"Yup, now we gots an army officer, a sheriff, his daughter,

and my niece all coming to our war dance. Rocky Feller in custody of army now." He spent another fifteen minutes bringing Stan Brown up to date.

"I hope somebody's smart enough to shoot a deer or it's gonna be a long hungry ride back. Let's go get that sumbitch."

The sun was bright and warm as they began their climb up through the rocks and brush, trying to be as quiet as possible. The brush was wet, snow still clinging to it, and the rocks were icy and slick as hot bear grease. Dancing Antelope moved fast and quiet, his moccasins giving good footing while Brownie did a bit of skating and dancing in the slick spots with his western boots not up to the challenge.

Curly Joe Simpson was awakened by the smell of boiling coffee and cussed long and loud when he looked down the hill and spotted smoke coming from where he had tied off his horse. "Who is it that's following me? And drinking my coffee? I thought I killed that man yesterday. I know I heard him yell some when I shot."

Simpson's teeth were chattering he was so cold and there wasn't anything around him, trapped as he was in the high rocks, that he could burn. He checked his rifle and revolver, made sure both were fully loaded, and jumped up and down several times, trying to get warm. His fingers were stiff and hurt and, when he looked at his right hand, it was more gray in color than pink.

He quickly opened a button loop on his heavy coat and shoved his hand inside under his armpit, almost whining at the pain. "Frostbite," he whimpered. He tried to see into the area where his horse was, where the man had a fire going, and couldn't. He could see the smoke and smell the coffee but couldn't see anything. He wanted to run, but where? How could he get over this mountain range, still towering hundreds of feet above his little rock pile?

Simpson was looking around for a way out, some way that he could get away from this man chasing him, and heard the distinct sound of rocks being kicked about. Brownie had slipped in the ice and kicked some rocks catching his balance. Simpson zeroed in on where the sound came from and scrunched down into a crouch, rifle at the ready.

Come on you bastard, show yourself. Show yourself like you did yesterday and I'll put a chunk of lead through your fat head. If he could kill this man, he could get back to his horse; he'd be safe. "There," he murmured, raising the rifle quickly, but Brownie scurried behind an outcrop and was out of sight. Simpson had the rifle butt pushed hard into his shoulder, his finger twitching in his desire to kill that man.

Brownie jumped from his hiding place and took two steps to disappear behind another large rock and Simpson couldn't pull the trigger. His finger wouldn't move and when he looked at his hand, he found his finger wasn't even on the trigger, it was outside and on the rim of the trigger guard. It wouldn't move. He had no feeling. He tried again, again, and couldn't get his finger to respond.

He was howling in anger and pain when he heard a quiet voice behind him say, "Better be quiet, stupid man. Somebody might hear," and then everything went black. Dancing Antelope caught the rifle after smashing Simpson in the back of the head with his pistol butt, and let the man fall to the ground.

"Come on up, Brown Man. Curly Joe taking nap."

Three men were sitting around a big fire, two of them enjoying plates full of bacon and cups full of coffee, when they heard a "Halloo the camp" come from the ridge of the gulch they were in.

"Got company, Brown Man," Dancing Antelope said. He jumped up and scrambled to the top of the arroyo to welcome Corcoran and the posse. "Good you make it. We got Curly Joe and he all angry at us and Rocky Feller."

The group scrambled down into the arroyo and tied off their horses. "Good sign you left for us, Dancing Antelope. Thank you," Terrence Corcoran said. Schultz and Buckmaster were ripping out more sage and brush for the fire and Betsy and Chasing Rabbits got the remainder of their food supplies warming along with another pot of coffee boiling. It was a busy camp on a bright autumn morning.

"Well, Curly Joe," Corcoran said, squatting next to the outlaw, "it's a real pleasure to see you again. Let's you and me have a nice little talk. I'll ask a question or two and you'll give me the answers. You understand how that works, right?" Curly Joe didn't answer and Corcoran's big right hand came out fast and slapped the outlaw across the side of his face.

"I thought you knew how the game was played. Well, let's try again. Remember now, I ask, you answer. What gave you the idea to create the homestead fraud?"

"Ain't no fraud. The man walked off, told me the place was mine if I wanted it."

Simpson was sitting cross-legged in front of the fire, Corcoran on his haunches next to him. Without the slightest warning, a heavy fist slammed into the side of Simpson's head, sending the man sprawling into the snow and mud. "Who put you up to it, Curly Joe? You ain't smart enough to come up with something like this. We got us a long ride back to Sheriff Schultz's little jail, Curly Joe, and I'm gonna put a fist to the side of your head every time you don't give me an answer.

"Nate Coppersmith did not ride off his ranch and tell you it was yours if you wanted it. The plan to coerce that man into thinking you would maintain his homestead while he took care of his family was well thought out and planned. Someone far smarter than you was behind that plan, Curly Joe. Who was it?"

"I got nothin' to say to you. I own that ranch, own that homestead claim, and Reg Chapman signed the papers himself. Go to hell, Corcoran." He cried out when the fist splashed his nose across his broad face and couldn't use his frostbitten hand to wipe the blood away. "I'll kill you," he stammered.

"Sure you will, Simpson. What was in that letter that brought you up to this country? Who was that letter from?"

"What?" He scrambled to his feet, his eyes wild with fear. "Letter? How ... ?" and he sat back down by the fire, head down, eyes closed, waiting for the next blow. Corcoran walked over to where Schultz and Betsy were talking.

"Looks like Rockefeller knew what he was talking about. He's all yours, Sheriff."

"I heard all that. Good job. I wonder if we'll find that letter cuz I'll betcha the farm he won't say who sent it or what it said."

"The next time you want to hit him, let me do it, Terrence," Betsy said "He laughed when that other big ape slugged me and Chasing Rabbits said he laughed every time Rockefeller hit her." He had to smile watching her fold and unfold her fists and was willing to concede that she could do some damage.

They ate well, drank lots of coffee, and emptied what little was left in the flask before Corcoran said it was time to get back on the trail. "It's gonna be a long, cold two or three days getting back. Dancing Antelope, can you see what kind of game you can find? We'll need meat and lots of it to make this trek. Let's saddle up."

CHAPTER FIFTEEN

The news that Pete Peters had been arrested by the army spread through Winnemucca like a range fire and Nate Coppersmith was at the sheriff's office as soon as he heard. "Sam, tell me about it. What happened?"

Chief Deputy Sam Messing, now acting sheriff of Humboldt County, still had the look of a frightened rabbit when Coppersmith barged in. "Peters must have known that Curly Joe Simpson was a wanted man and didn't do anything about it, Nate. I'm sorry, but he never showed us those wanted sheets."

"I'm at a loss," Coppersmith said. "Why is the army involved? Why did Peters even ride north to Fort McDermott?"

"That Rocky Rockefeller beat up Betsy Schultz and Simpson shot an army trooper at the Indian village. That's what the deputy assigned to the fort told me. He said when Captain Watson found out the two men were wanted outlaws that he was going to hang our sheriff. He had our deputy, Aural Douglas, send a message demanding Peters report to the fort immediately."

Messing took a rag from his pocket and wiped his face. "Nate, I wish there was something I could say or do. None of this should have been allowed."

"And that's exactly what Captain Watson said. None of this, you losing the ranch and herd, Betsy being beat up, and the trooper shot." He took a long breath, got up and walked over to the stove and poured a cup of hot coffee. "None of it, Nate. None of it would have happened if Peters had done his job. Peters came right out and admitted that he had held back the information in the wanted posters."

"He must've been involved right from the beginning, Sam." Coppersmith was just pacing around the small office, shaking his head in frustration. "I want whoever is involved, whether it's Chapman, Peters, whoever, put in prison or shot dead.

"What should I do now, Sam? Am I ever getting my ranch back? My finest steers have been sold, my wife can't stop crying. Damn Pete Peters."

"The Army's gonna hang Peters, I think," Messing said. "Everyone knows what a sadistic bastard Watson is and he looked almost gleeful when he put Peters under arrest. I'm afraid the sheriff's days are numbered."

Coppersmith wanted to dance and sing but didn't have an opportunity as Seamus Doherty burst into the small office, a broad smile across his face. "Good news travels fast, Nate. Me and Susan were about to head back to the ranch when Messing and the deputies rode in. You okay, Sam?"

"Yeah, Watson didn't believe me when I said Peters never showed us the posters but he didn't arrest me either. What are you going to do now, Nate?"

"I don't know. I don't know if Simpson is still at the ranch. I don't know where Corcoran is. I just don't know."

"Corcoran?" Messing sat straight up in his chair. No one

had mentioned that Doherty and Coppersmith had Corcoran working for them. "Terrence Corcoran? He's involved in this?" He just shook his head in wonder. "I rode with Corcoran on a couple of chases but I'd never believe he'd tie up with someone like Curly Joe Simpson."

"No, no," Doherty said. He was laughing at the thought. "No, Sam, Terrence is working for Nate to get his ranch back but we haven't heard from him for some time now." He looked around the small office, at the walls, ceiling, and floor, in deep thought. He finally made up his mind not to say anything to this newly appointed sheriff about how they were working to get Nate's ranch back. He knew that he had no idea who's side Messing might be on despite what Messing had said.

"I think we need to find a cold beer somewhere, Nate, and get this all figured out."

"I'll buy," is all Coppersmith said, walking toward the door. "Thank you for being honest with me, Sam. I appreciate that." Doherty still had those thoughts about who's side Messing was on, Peters' or Coppersmith's?

It was a quiet afternoon at the Star Saloon and Restaurant when the two walked in. "Give us a couple with a good head," Seamus said. "We'll be at the window table." They got settled, the barman was quick with the beer, and Nate could feel every nerve in his body screwed down as tight as they would go.

The Star Saloon was in the very center of Winnemucca with the south facing bat-wing doors opening onto the east-west emigrant trail and a set of doors on the east wall opening onto the northbound trail to Fort McDermott and Oregon country. It was an elegant saloon serving the finest liquors money could buy, had honest gaming tables, and served some of the finest beef and lamb in central Nevada.

"Do you think Peters was behind all this? The deputies weren't told the sheriff allowed known outlaws to steal my ranch and did nothing? My God, Seamus. Can I just ride out and take my ranch back? What do I do?" He fired those thoughts and questions as fast as a gunman fanning a Colt.

"First, old man, slow down," Doherty chuckled. "No, I don't think you should go anywhere near that place right now. Until we hear from Corcoran, we have to stay out of whatever is happening. Keep in mind that you believe Peters to be involved but I and others also have our doubts about land agent Chapman.

"If there has been a conspiracy, whoever was working with Simpson is going to show himself, to take control. From what Messing said, gang member Rockefeller is in custody and Simpson is on the run. We don't want to frighten off whoever else is involved nor do we want to get in their sights if they are killers like Simpson."

"I guess you're right," Coppersmith said. He didn't want to say that, didn't want to finish his beer. He wanted to get on his horse and ride to his ranch. He wanted to help Susan pack up the children and follow him. The sadness was almost overwhelming.

"What if Simpson isn't at the ranch? What about the cattle, hogs, sheep? Somebody has to be there." There were too many unanswered questions, too many things that could go wrong, and Coppersmith sat with a cold beer, helpless. For one of the few times in his life, the huge man was able to do nothing.

"I can't just sit around and do nothing, Seamus. I'm so ashamed of myself. I let that foul outlaw take that ranch right out from under me like I was a lamb led to slaughter."

"Until we know where Terrence Corcoran is and what is

happening with Simpson and his gang, we have to sit around and do nothing; otherwise, we'll be adding to the chaos. What if Chapman's involved too, Nate? We have to stay away from that ranch until we have some answers. This was a well planned out assault, Nate, a plan that someone like Simpson couldn't carry out on his own.

"Just as Captain Watson seemed unwilling to believe that Sheriff Peters didn't inform his deputies that the Curly Joe Simpson gang had taken over your ranch, that wanted outlaws were living the good life at your expense, I'm not sure I believe it either. Get you anger and frustration under control, old man. It's time for some deep thinking, not just reaction. We need to know a lot more than we do before we can actually do anything."

A tired, hungry, and cold group of riders were tying off their horses in front of the Golden Gulch Saloon in Grant County, Oregon. It was close to the noon hour, a brilliant late fall sun shining down on still fresh snow and, for the first time in two days, no wind was howling through the high mountain desert. Simpson, bleeding from his encounters with Corcoran, Brownie, and Buckmaster, had to be helped from his horse.

After Corcoran's comments about a letter, the outlaw hadn't said a word to anyone which made Corcoran even more anxious to know what it contained and who might have sent it. Corcoran and Schultz spent some time discussing whether or not they believed Simpson was smart enough to come up with the plan to steal the ranch on his own.

"Go on in and get yourselves warm," David Schultz said. "I'll take old Curly Joe here to the lock-up and join you in a couple of minutes."

"I'll walk with you, Sheriff," Lt. Buckmaster said. "That way we will maintain equal jurisdiction over this piece of

crap. I'll have to show in my report that he was always in my
custody." The two men were still trying to work out who
would maintain full custody of the prisoner. Was he Oregon's
man or did he belong to the army?

While those three walked off, Betsy took Corcoran by the
arm and led him into the

warmth of the saloon, nodding to Chasing Rabbits to
follow. "I'm so tired I could sleep for a week," she said.
"What happens now, Terrence? Can Susan and Nate take
their ranch back?" She'd asked the question often and not
gotten a response and the look in her eye told Corcoran he'd
better say something this time.

"I'll be hanged if I can figure out whether Simpson had
help in this conspiracy or not, Betsy. If he did, then Nate
needs to stay away from the ranch until we can prove that
Simpson has vacated the homestead claim. Was he in cahoots
with the sheriff? With the land agent? Or with both?" He
warmed his hands by the red-hot potbelly stove and looked
into the charming lady's eyes. The loveliest eyes I've seen in
many years, he thought, and such a beautiful smile. What a
wonder to waken to that smile every morning. I'm a travelin'
man, but I might be convinced to hang up that old pack of
mine and put the mule out to pasture.

He put an arm around Betsy and drew her in close, could
feel the warmth of her, wanted to feel the taste of her. "We'll
find an answer, Shaggy Hair. We will." He was putting
together a plan to draw out the co-conspirator if there was
one. "Tomorrow, I think Dancing Antelope and I will need to
return to the ranch and make sure everything is in order."

"Then what?" she asked, not trying to pull away from his
strong arms. She nestled in tight, felt the great strength of
the man, closed her eyes, but still worried about Susan and
Nate, and their ranch. "What will you be expecting? I feel
you're putting yourself up as a target, Terrence."

"No, not a target, but the word will get out that Simpson has fled and his gang with him, and that might draw out his partner if there is one. Then we'll have legal authority to do something about Nate Coppersmith's homestead claim."

"You like the idea of going back to the ranch, don't you? Have you ever thought about having one of your own? Running some fine beef and hogs? Or have you been fully satisfied being a lawman?"

Corcoran pulled her closer, felt her strong body nestled warmly against his and didn't answer for several moments. "I've worked some on a ranch or two but never had one of my own. It takes some hard work, a man needs a strong woman at his side," he said softly and looked into those bright eyes. "Can't think about things like that, not with Nate and his wife about to lose their ranch. I got to keep focused, Betsy, but I think we do need to carry this conversation on some. Just not right now."

"What can I do to help? I want to help, Terrence, and you know I'm capable." He drew his arms tighter, her aroma flooding his system, and bent down to kiss her. She offered up her face and two big men coughed loudly from behind them.

"You are in public, you know," Brownie laughed, and Dancing Antelope tried to pretend he was hiding his eyes. The barman whooped in laughter watching Corcoran and Shaggy Hair stand in embarrassment, but not until their lips met and electricity flowed.

"Everyone have your fun. We're discussing some serious business," Betsy said and Terrence knew immediately that was the wrong thing to say. The taunts and teasing, laughter, and wild comments brought her to the point she hid her head in his chest, his arms still tightly around her.

She asked all the right questions and I wanted to give her the answers she wants to hear. Terrence, old man, you better be damn cautious. Damn caution, because I really do want her and a ranch and big old place like Seamus and Meagan have.

"I could hear you all clear across the street," Schultz said as he and Buckmaster returned from locking Simpson up. "What did I miss? Betsy?" and he saw her clinging to Corcoran, hiding her head. "What have you done?" He knew his daughter well enough to know she probably was at the bottom of all this laughter and hooting.

"So," Corcoran said. "Simpson is all locked up and safe?"

"Nice try, Corcoran. Spill it, Betsy," Schultz laughed, seeing the two, still locked in a hug, tinged in red.

"I let my emotions get the better of me, David. I apologize," Corcoran said. Betsy slowly slipped out of his long arms and stood straight and tall, proud as all get-out, and gave her father a grand smile.

"He was a perfect gentleman, Daddy. Now, let's talk about how we get Susan's and Nate's ranch back for them. Corcoran has a plan."

"I bet he does," Brownie laughed. "It may even include Coppersmith's ranch."

The laughter was broken up by the sound of a rider coming down the main street at a hard gallop, pulling up in front of the sheriff's office. Schultz ran out the door, Brownie and Corcoran right behind him. A single army trooper was jumping from his horse as they raced across the street. The man was covered in ice and mud, his horse covered in icy flecks of foam and mud. "Lieutenant Buckmaster here?" He yelled it out, jumping from the tired pony.

Lt. Buckmaster was the last one out the door and caught up with the group as they all hurried into the small sheriff's office. "What do you have, trooper?"

"Sir," the man said, snapping to attention. "Dispatch from Captain Watson, sir."

"Thank you. Let's all go back to the saloon and get warm."

He opened the dispatch held in a leather pouch as they trooped back to the Golden Gulch. "Seems I'm ordered to return to Fort McDermott immediately. Humboldt County Sheriff Peters has been arrested on charges including neglect of duty."

He, Schultz, and Corcoran were grouped around the stove as he read the message. "You better bring us up to date, Corporal. What's going on at the fort?"

"Your patrol brought their prisoner in, a man named James Rockefeller, and they were followed by a trader named Peabody who told Captain Watson the story Betsy Schultz had told him about the Coppersmith ranch.

"The captain demanded that Sheriff Peters come to the post and tell him why these men had not been arrested. Captain Watson then arrested the sheriff. Begging the lieutenant's pardon, the post is in an uproar, sir. Captain Watson is looking for blood."

"As well as I," Corcoran snapped. The news of Sheriff Peters under arrest changed Corcoran's timeline quickly. Word may already have reached Winnemucca.

"I'm leaving with Dancing Antelope as soon as we have something to eat. We'll maintain the ranch." He looked around the saloon and called out. "Betsy, can you ride to Winnemucca to find the Coppersmiths and bring them up to date on what's happened so far?

"When the word gets out, if Curly Joe Simpson had a partner in this scheme, he will want to be at that ranch pronto. To maintain the claim. And Dancing Antelope and I will take him out. When you find Coppersmith, have him take you to a man named Seamus Doherty and tell him the same story."

Corcoran just made himself more and more angry thinking of all the trouble this fiasco was going to be for Nate Coppersmith. *Can he reclaim the ranch? Will the feds even allow that? Who, besides Simpson, is involved? This can't be just one dumb-ass outlaw riding in out of nowhere and creating this homestead claim jumping. He has to have had help from somewhere. Someone gave him the idea and helped him finish it and I'm gonna grind that bastard into desert dust. If I find out it's Peters, I hope that tin star has sharp edges when I shove it up his arse.*

CHAPTER SIXTEEN

Betsy helped Corcoran pack a few things to take back to the ranch with him and walked him to his horse. "I'll ride to the village this afternoon and then into Winnemucca tomorrow morning, Terrence. I've met Seamus Doherty and his wife Meagan. They are wonderful people. You stay safe, mister," she said. He bent down in the saddle and gave her a long kiss, kicked old Rube lightly, and trotted off toward the Sleepy U. Dancing Antelope was riding right alongside with a chuckle and wicked smile.

"You just mind your manners, buddy," Corcoran said but couldn't wipe the smile from his face.

"That trail's gonna be a busy one, Betsy." David Schultz had his arm around his daughter watching Corcoran ride south. "Lieutenant Buckmaster and the corporal will ride to the village with you in an hour or so, then onto the fort tomorrow. Are you sure you want to do this? It could get dangerous, girl."

"I've already been beat up by one outlaw, Dad. I have to

do this. Susan Coppersmith is the best friend I've ever had. Those children need their ranch, and Nate is getting the best help possible from Corcoran. Yes, Dad, I have to."

"I'll help you put together a good kit. Make sure you pack extra food and water when you ride out for Winnemucca. Don't get caught short like we did last week. Riding out without extra food was stupid and someone should shoot me for putting you in danger like that."

"We thought it was a quick ride to the ranch, Dad. Did it ever enter anyone's mind that we would be chasing outlaws for sixty miles or so? Don't blame yourself." She stopped short, looked all around the saloon. "Have you seen Chasing Rabbits? She needs to get home, too."

"She put a blanket down behind the potbelly and has slept through all the racket and chaos," Schultz laughed. "Let's get you ready to ride, then wake her."

An hour later and Lt. Buckmaster led the group out of town toward the village. Chasing Rabbits elected to ride a horse for the return trip and the young cavalry corporal went out of his way to be her escort. Chasing Rabbits' command of the English language almost didn't exist and the corporal's family was from Bavaria so his accent was rather guttural and heavy. Betsy spent a great deal of time laughing at the two trying to hold a conversation.

It was more than obvious the young man enjoyed the company of a young woman with flashing brown eyes and long black hair. She seemed to be taken with blue eyes and long blond hair. "Ah, sweet young love," she murmured through thoughts of Terrence Corcoran's green eyes and long reddish hair.

Those thoughts also kept her from having to put up with the lieutenant's desire to be friendly. Little wind, a warm day, and the ride to the village was most pleasant. Buckmaster met with his unit and made ready to ride to Fort McDermott the next morning. Betsy packed for her venture into Winnemucca but was interrupted by a visit from the trader, Henry Peabody.

"We've been worried, Betsy. Glad you're back safe. Is that Simpson fellow dead?"

What a strange question, she thought; why would he ask that? "Come in, Mr. Peabody. Would you like a cup of coffee? I'm packing for Winnemucca but I'd be glad to put a pot on."

"I don't want to take up your valuable time but I would like to hear what happened on your chase." She already had her stove fired up and she put a pot of coffee together quickly and joined Peabody at the table to tell of the chase into Oregon.

"So, your father has him in custody, eh? With that trooper dead and the wanted posters we've heard about, I would think he would have been killed on sight."

Betsy's mind was quick and she remembered what Corcoran had told her would happen as soon as the word spread that Simpson was in custody. If he had a partner, he said that partner would make for the ranch to insure the claim. *I think I just found Curly Joe's partner. I'm not going to Winnemucca, I'm going to the ranch, and I'm going right now.*

She did her best to hustle Peabody out of her little apartment behind the schoolroom, packed quickly for the ride to the Sleepy U ranch. "I won't tell anyone that I'm not going to Winnemucca. That's why Peabody was sitting with Simpson and Rockefeller in the trading post. Simpson was going to sell the ranch to Peabody." She was murmuring to herself a mile a minute as she tied off the small pack.

She stopped short as she walked out the door to leave. "Somebody has to get word to Winnemucca. Someone needs to tell Nate and Doherty. Damn," she whispered, blushing just a bit. She hurried the three hundred yards or so to where the army had their small encampment and

asked one of the troopers to take her to Lieutenant
Buckmaster.

"He asked not to be disturbed, miss," the orderly said
when they arrived at Buckmaster's tent.

"This is far more important than anything he might be
doing," she said. "It has everything to do with our recent
chase across the desert. Now tell him I'm here, please."

The orderly was back with the young officer in minutes
and Betsy took Buckmaster by the arm and walked him away
from where others might hear. "Remember Corcoran talking
about ferreting out a possible Simpson partner?"

"Indeed," he said. "That was the purpose of you going to
town and he going back to the ranch. You look upset, Betsy.
What's happened?"

"When Simpson and Rockefeller came to the village, they
were in a meeting with Henry Peabody when he called for me
to come tend to Rockefeller's wounds. That's when Rockefeller attacked me and Simpson shot the soldier. They were at
that meeting so Peabody could buy the Sleepy U ranch." She
took a long breath and looked deep into Buckmaster's eyes
before she continued.

"Peabody just came to my apartment and the first thing
he asked was whether or not Simpson had been killed. The
second thing he asked was where Simpson was being held.
Peabody has to be Simpson's partner and I have to tell
Corcoran."

"Yes," Buckmaster agreed. "Corcoran needs to be told
immediately." Buckmaster paced around the little area they
were in, coming to a halt in front of Betsy. "Somebody needs
to tell your father, too."

"And Nate Coppersmith. Don't forget them, Lieutenant.
God, what a mess."

"I've been ordered to return to McDermott but I have
soldiers at my command, Betsy. Here's what we have to do.

I'll send a trooper to warn your father that Peabody or someone might try to bust Simpson out or kill him. Another trooper can ride to Winnemucca and give the good news to Coppersmith and Doherty, and you ride to Corcoran and let him know."

"If that can be done, can we keep it just between all of us? We don't want Peabody to know what we're doing." It was Betsy's turn to pace around through the dust for a minute or two.

"No, we don't want him to know what we're doing and we don't have enough information to arrest him either. I want you to take some time and write out in plain talk what you told me. Make two letters, one to your father, one to Coppersmith, and I'll get two of my best men to make the rides.

"Bring those letters to me as quickly as you can get them on paper, then ride fast to Corcoran. I'll take care of this end."

She threw her arms around the surprised officer to the great delight of several enlisted men standing nearby and rushed back to her apartment. The letters were written and delivered, her horse packed and saddled, and Betsy was out of the village within the hour. Anyone watching would have seen two soldiers, packed for a trip, leaving town as well, one heading toward Oregon, one toward Winnemucca.

Nate and Susan Coppersmith had accepted the invitation from Seamus Doherty to bring the children to his ranch for a long stay. "Until we get all this straightened out, I'm going to do my best to keep you out of trouble, my friend," Seamus laughed. "I, too, want someone's blood, Nate, but I want it done properly and legally. Whoever it is behind Curly Joe's plan to steal your ranch is smart and cagey. We have to be smarter and far more cagey."

"I understand all that, Seamus, I really do. It's just that I have feelings that go soul-deep about that ranch and my family. I'll do as you say. I know Corcoran is a good man and he'll do everything possible to get my ranch back." He sat on the sofa, jumped to his feet, and sat back down. "Why haven't we heard anything?"

Seamus Doherty shook his head, almost chuckled at the question. He wondered what it was he was expecting, maybe a rider coming in on a flying horse proclaiming all is well. The man wants miracles and he's going to be more than lucky if he gets his ranch back sometime in the next five years.

"We have, Nate. Sheriff Peters is in custody, Rockefeller is in custody. And Corcoran is chasing Simpson. Now, old man, you calm yourself, have a hot brandy by the fire with me, and listen to your children playing outside and your wife helping Meagan in the kitchen."

Coppersmith had to chuckle at the way Doherty calmed him down, smiled at his long-time friend, and offered his cup for a refill. "A man couldn't ask for a better friend, Seamus. Thank you. I've always wanted things done yesterday; why are things always so slow to get done, why wasn't that herd brought down before the snow, why are those steers not already branded. It's just the way I am. I want Corcoran to ride into this ranch today and hand me the keys to my ranch."

Both men laughed just a bit, settled down in the comfort of leather-covered chairs by a warm fire with brandies in hand. Late fall in Paradise Valley was a lovely place to be and Coppersmith was aware that, despite all his troubles, he was lucky to have a friend like Seamus Doherty.

"It's a two-day ride from here to your ranch going cross country through the Quinn River country and the Pueblo Valley, barring storms. If what we heard from Sam Messing about the sheriff is true, we might get a visitor tomorrow. Either Corcoran or a message from him. You have to believe that the word about Peters being arrested by the army will spread through this county like a wind-driven range fire."

Just as Doherty said, two days later a rider was seen coming down the long trail into the ranch. "Looks like a cavalry trooper, Seamus," Meagan said. The Coppersmith's and Doherty's were on the porch enjoying a late morning coffee when Corporal Helmut Heinz rode up to the hitching post.

"Good morning," he said. "I'm looking for Seamus Doherty."

"I'm Doherty. What can I do for you, soldier?"

"I have a letter for you, sir. And could you tell me how to locate a man named Nathaniel Coppersmith. I have a message for him as well."

"I'm Coppersmith," Nate said.

Heinz was off his horse and on the porch in three strides, handing Betsy's letters to the men. Nothing was said until both men had read what she wrote. "This is splendid news, Seamus," Nate said. He handed the letter to Susan to read. "Maybe we can return to our ranch soon."

"It is good news, Nate, but there's a big warning spelled out here. No, we cannot return to your ranch. Not yet. I read danger all over this letter. That trader Peabody has a bad reputation in Idaho, in Nevada, probably even in Utah. It's always surprised me that he was able to run a trading post in that little village.

"Corcoran just might have his hands full for a while longer." Doherty ushered everyone into the big house, including the soldier, and had them sit around the fire. "Did you stop in Winnemucca?" he asked Heinz.

"Yes sir. I asked the sheriff where I could find you and Mr. Coppersmith. Lieutenant Buckmaster made it clear that no one but who the letters were addressed to should be made aware of the problem so all I asked for were directions." He took an offered cup of coffee from Meagan and sat stiffly near the fire.

"Good," Seamus said. "But Sam Messing isn't ignorant and will put two and two together quickly. He'll know something's up, Nate." Doherty looked at the soldier for just a minute before continuing. "How much of all of this are you aware, Corporal Heinz?"

Corporal Heinz spelled out the initial problem when Simpson and Rockefeller came to the village and was a member of the patrol that brought Rockefeller to the village. He was also the man who brought Buckmaster's orders to return to McDermott and helped escort Betsy and Chasing Rabbits back to the village. With some urging from Doherty, Heinz told about Corcoran's chase across the desert and the capture of Simpson.

"If Peabody was acting alone, Corcoran will have him in irons soon," Seamus said. "If he has a gang behind him, this could get nasty. What are your orders, Corporal Heinz?"

"I'm to return to the village until the lieutenant gets back with our orders, sir."

"Good. Nate, you and I will escort this fine soldier back to the village tomorrow morning.

Meagan, will you and Susan make up a good kit for the three of us? We will want to eat well and have the necessary liquid refreshment to make our evening camps somewhat pleasurable."

Heinz had a good smile on his face as he warmed his hands by the fire.

Meagan's tinkle of laughter lit up the great room even more than Nate Coppersmith's smile.

"Thank you, Seamus," is all he said.

CHAPTER SEVENTEEN

Betsy put her horse in a strong trot for the ride to the Sleepy U, checking about every five minutes or so on the Remington she had tucked in her waist sash and behind her for anyone following. She didn't see Peabody when she left the village and didn't notice anyone paying any particular attention to her leaving. Still, those men were known murderers and Peabody was partners with them. Was he one too?

"It's strange, though," she muttered, "that it was Peabody who attended to my wounds when that big ape attacked me. It was Peabody who alerted the soldiers about the attack. Was he protecting himself? Did he already get what he wanted from Simpson?" The only thing she knew for sure was she was riding to Terrence Corcoran. With that thought, she touched her fast mare with her spurs.

Fear coupled with anger alongside thoughts of Corcoran kept her moving forward at a fast pace along with the fact that she knew almost nothing of Henry Peabody. Was he a criminal like Simpson? Did he have a gang of outlaws? Why would the man who operated the village trading post partner up with a bank robber and killer? Too many questions and too few answers.

"Even if Peabody isn't a murderer, he's a vile man for making all this happen to Susan Coppersmith," she muttered. Her anger had been growing ever since she was sure she discovered Simpson's partner and she knew she would shoot Peabody on sight. She was running out of daylight and was still several miles from the ranch when she noticed dust off to her right.

"Whoever that is, is riding quiet but at a solid trot. I wonder if he's on a trail that connects with this one. Let's go, big girl," she said, touching spurs to her fast horse and putting it in a solid lope for the final miles into the ranch. Whoever was riding at an angle toward her must have seen her horse speed up but she saw right away that he didn't.

She never slowed the big horse down until she rode into the barnyard and up to the well-lit kitchen porch. She jumped down and tied off quickly and was about to run up the stairs when first, the kitchen door opened and second, Dancing Antelope came riding in at a fast trot.

"You been in a big hurry, Shaggy Hair," he laughed. "Thought you were in Winnemucca. Look what I found, Terrence."

Corcoran was standing at the kitchen door with a frown that could have been seen across the barnyard. "What's the problem, Betsy?" He held the door as she hurried into the warmth of the Sleepy U ranch kitchen. "Why aren't you heading for Coppersmith's?"

"Let me catch my breath, Terrence," she said. He held a chair for her while Dancing Antelope got three cups filled with hot coffee. She didn't want to sit down; she wanted to throw her arms around Corcoran and feel safe. "I think I accidentally found out who Curly Joe's partner is, Terrence.

The trader Henry Peabody almost has to be the man who set all this in motion."

Betsy Schultz spent the next hour telling the story of Peabody and how Buckmaster sent riders to her father and to Coppersmith and Doherty. Corcoran had a million questions when she finally stopped talking. "Good work, Betsy. Did you notice whether Peabody was still in the village when you left?"

She shook her head. "I'm pretty sure no one followed me either. The only other rider I saw must have been you, Dancing Antelope."

"There were two men about a mile behind you, Shaggy Hair, but when they saw my dust they turned around. It was getting dark so I followed you in. Maybe I should have followed them."

"No," Corcoran said. "You did the right thing. But just in case they didn't really go back, let's prepare for visitors. What do you know about this Peabody fellow?" he asked Dancing Antelope.

"Not much except he willing to cheat. He change prices, doesn't give full measure, and you don't want to hire one of his wagons to haul for you. Yup, maybe not bank robber, but him good cheat."

Corcoran walked out, motioning the two to follow him. "We'll get your stuff inside, Betsy, then put the horses up. We'll leave Dancing Antelope's horse saddled, though. If we have to chase somebody, we'll have a little head start that way."

"Let's keep the fire up in the kitchen stove and just one lamp burning low," Dancing Antelope said. "I never did trust that trader. He always kinda slick with the dollars and make change too fast. Faster than Indian can count. He bought a ranch in Idaho little time ago, you know.

"Maybe had help there, too. Make good dollars if you help

someone steal a ranch, then buy it from them for nickels and then sell for dollars. You say he was offering to buy this ranch from Simpson? Now he very interested to know Simpson is dead. Yup, Corcoran, he be here soon."

"You said you saw two riders following Betsy. I wonder if it was Peabody or men who work for him. How many people work at that trading post?"

"Only a couple," Betsy answered. "He also has a freight business and runs wagons between Grant County and Boise, and between Winnemucca and Boise. He could have ten or twelve men available, Terrence."

"No worry then," Corcoran laughed. "I've got Shaggy Hair and Dancing Antelope on my side." That brought a chuckle from the Paiute and a frown from Betsy. "Let's make sure all our guns are loaded and we know where all our ammo is. This is a big house with too many windows and too many ways in and out."

The main house was built in a Spanish style which allowed for each bedroom to have an outside entrance, the great room had one, the sitting room had one and, of course, the kitchen had one.

"Maybe we defend this place from bunkhouse, Corcoran."

"Just one more reason why I like you, Dancing Antelope. Betsy, you're in charge of seeing to it that we have plenty of food and water. Dancing Antelope you see to it that we have gun ports at each of the windows and the doors can be barricaded."

"That's fine," Betsy almost snarled. "Woman's work, eh? Food and water, as if I can't fight. What does that leave you to do?"

"If you'd rather cut gun ports, that's fine. Dancing Antelope, you bring food and water. I'm going to see to it that if we do get company, we'll know it in enough time to do something about it."

"I'm sorry, Corcoran. I wasn't thinking. I'll take care of food and water. I just don't like being forced to do woman things. I'm a better fighter."

"You'll get your chance to fight." He smiled and slipped an arm around her. "You do just fine at doing woman things, too," and he bent to kiss her when he heard the hiss from Dancing Antelope. "And you mind your own business," he laughed.

In less then an hour, the windows were set up for good defense. "I think old Nate Coppersmith may have had trouble in the past around here. This place is already set up for defense," Corcoran said. The shutters could be closed and offered portholes large enough for a rifle barrel to be pushed through and the shooter able to sight. There were tables alongside each window for ammunition and extra weapons.

"Big trouble around here when Bannok's were angry. Nate lost his home when it burned." Dancing Antelope said.

Betsy had a store of food and water in the bunkhouse. She and Dancing Antelope had mattresses stacked along the walls near the windows to stop bullets coming through the thin wood walls. They had only one kerosene lamp burning and it was near the wood stove which burned hot. There was a good supply of firewood nearby.

"I think we're set. Where's Corcoran?" Betsy walked toward the door just as the big man came in. "Where you been?" She had her fists resting comfortably on her hips demanding an answer.

"Seeing to it we know it if we get visitors," is all he said. He was chuckling as he poured a cup of boiling coffee. "Ease off a little, Shaggy Hair. You're strung up pretty tight and all you're gonna do is make yourself tired. If Peabody has people, it will take a bit of time before he can get organized enough to hit us. Fact is, he'd probably go after Simpson before us. He doesn't want that man to be alive."

She walked over to him and let him fold her into his strong arms. "I'm sorry," she whispered. "I haven't been in this kind of situation since I was a little girl." He held her tight, rocked back and forth for a moment or two, and kissed her on top of her head. "I could stay just like this for the rest of my life."

Corcoran had those same thoughts but didn't say so. He just held her nice and tight, enjoying the moment and knew they would be in a big fight very soon. At the end of it, he hoped, Nate Coppersmith would have his ranch back.

"You're sure you were followed?" Sheriff David P. Schultz was sitting behind his desk looking into the eyes of a dust-covered Crazy Dog, the tracker for the Fort McDermott Cavalry. He read the letter again that Crazy Dog had brought. "Peabody." He had said that twice before. "This is most strange."

Schultz walked to the stove and poured some coffee. "Are you supposed to return to the village?"

"No. Lieutenant Buckmaster said could stay with you if you need me. I good fighter, Sheriff."

"I bet you are," Schultz chuckled. He was looking at a man close to six feet tall, probably less than four ounces of fat anywhere on him, and as lithe as a cougar. "We might very well be in for one, too. Are you aware of what's in this letter and why?"

"I believe so. Shaggy Hair good friend. She read me letter and I know why we first chased that man Simpson out of town. Yup, Sheriff, I know. That Simpson feller maybe hurt Chasing Rabbits. Peabody maybe help. I fight."

"Tell me about who was following you."

"Two riders followed me out of town and stayed about a mile behind all the way. If I make for fast, they do, too, and if I go slow, they do. Yup, they very much just follow Crazy

Dog. I made them go some hard places just for fun to watch. Not good horsemen."

"Okay." Schultz chuckled at the thought of the Indian leading the men into rocks and canyons just because he could. "Go across the street to the Golden Gulch Saloon and get something to eat and then you and Brownie come back here. We need to make some plans."

Schultz watched Crazy Dog walk toward the saloon and worried about whether he could keep Simpson safe. "Maybe I should have let the army take him back to McDermott. Peabody wouldn't attack the fort but he sure as hell might attack my little jail," he said to himself.

It was less than half an hour when Brownie and Crazy Dog returned. "Brownie, I know you've spent a long time in the saddle but I've got a job for you. See if you can round up four or five men from some of the surrounding ranches to come into town for a few days. Otherwise, it'll be just the three of us taking on whoever Peabody sends against us and those aren't good odds."

"Most of his teamsters have paper floating around, Sheriff. Outlaws hauling freight and casing the towns they haul to. I'll leave out at dawn and see what I can gather. I doubt he'll hit tonight."

CHAPTER EIGHTEEN

It was half an hour after leaving Betsy's schoolroom that Peabody realized what he had done. All the activity; Betsy almost running to the army enclave, then packing and riding out of town quickly; two soldiers packing and riding out in different directions; and Peabody knew he made a mistake.

"Bob," he called to a tall, thin man at the front of the trading post. "Come here. I need you, pard."

'Bob' was Waco Bob Torres, a notorious Texas gunman who served time at Huntsville and Carson City, and was driving wagons for Peabody to let things cool down some after a foray through a few of California's banks. His motto of 'no witnesses' had made his wanted posters declare 'dead or alive'. Peabody had his hands in half a dozen little groups of thieves and murderers and when they weren't carrying out jobs for him or others, they could find comfort, warmth, and safety with him.

Along with a freight business, Peabody was also involved in banking but not the traditional style preferred by most communities. He had operatives in several western states that kept him informed of gold, silver, and cash shipments to and from banks, and his gangs responded, relieving the shippers of their cargo. Waco Bob was a big part of those gangs.

"What's up, Peabody? I just got back from Boise. The mines might be easy pickin's but not the banks. They've been hit often and are like fortresses. We need to hit Salt Lake, Reno, or Virginia City, boss."

"That'll come. Right now, I want you to find Kimble, Floret, and Crandall. Get 'em here as quick as you can. We got a little problem."

"They got a camp a couple of miles out of town, Henry. Let's just ride out there." Waco Bob and Peabody made the fast ride and found the other teamsters sitting around a fire, passing a bottle back and forth. A small stream that started on the side of a hill not far distant as a bubbling spring gave them fresh water and cottonwood trees gave them shade and firewood.

"What's up, boss? You look a little riled." Jason Kimble was the only actual teamster of the bunch but Peabody also knew the man would back his play anytime he asked; Peabody had accidentally saved the man's mother one day and Kimble was more than grateful.

"I am riled. That damn ranch deal is about to blow up in my face. I need you men to keep that from happening."

"I told you that was a bad deal right from the start," Waco Bob said. "What's the problem?"

"Simpson and Rockefeller are in custody and neither one can keep his mouth shut. Rockefeller isn't smart enough to know what we did and he's at Fort McDermott so we can't worry about him.

"But that peacock Curly Joe will spill his guts the first time a fist slams the side of his head. He's being held at the Grant County jail. Don't get me wrong here, boys. I don't want that fool broke out; I want him dead."

"Hell, Henry, that's not a jail, it's a little wooden box. Me and Shorty can have Simpson's blood flowing anytime you want." Guy Floret was from the northwest wilds of Canada and was chased south by the Mounties several years before. He spoke with a distinct French accent, wore a tiny pencil moustache, and believed he was the answer to every woman's prayer.

Shorty Crandall, on the other hand, was a born killer; sadistic, ugly in mind and spirit, and lived on the thrill of danger. "You bet, Henry. One little flame and that jail would burn in a flash. Sure," Shorty laughed, "I'll be glad to kiss Curly Joe. Never did like that strutting little rooster."

"Good," Peabody said. "You and Guy kill Simpson. Kimble, you and Waco Bob ride with me to the Sleepy U ranch. I've got a bill of sale from Simpson and I've got to take possession of that place fast."

"That Indian, Dancing Antelope, is gonna be there. And that cowboy, Corcoran's his name," Waco Bob said. "I heard a couple of soldiers talking about him catching Simpson. Guess he thinks he's tough or something." There was general laughter around the fire.

"Don't have to be tough to catch a peacock like Curly Joe," Shorty Crandall laughed. "Just muss up his pretty clothes and he'll give up."

"Let's everybody be ready to ride come first light," Peabody said. "Bob, I want you to find somebody to ride to Boise and bring in a couple more guns, just in case. We've got people in Carson City, too; let's get word to them to join us here. We'll get this ranch thing straightened out, hit a couple of banks in Salt Lake, and move on to Denver.

"Any of you boys hear me say something about wanting to buy another ranch, just say Curly Joe, and I'll forget all about the idea." Laughter, a bottle of whiskey, and a warm fire were enjoyed by the group. Along with thoughts of dead lawmen.

"We should leave out right now, Henry," Waco Bob Torres

said. "We'd be at the ranch well before sunrise and catch them asleep."

"No, we'll do it my way," was all Peabody said. Waco Bob wasn't happy about that but didn't argue with the man.

"We clear that little rise in front of us, Seamus, and we'll look down on the prettiest little ranch in Nevada." Nate Coppersmith was having a hard time not putting his horse in a full-out, go for the gold run to the ranch. The two-day ride in from Paradise Valley had been an easy one, filled with talk of the future of the Sleepy U, rebuilding a good herd of beef, and expanding as the children grew older.

"I want you to stop thinking about what you might do in the future, Nate. Sometime in the next couple of hours it's more than likely we will be riding into a nest of outlaws, murderers, and thieves. Get your head squared around to that. Curly Joe Simpson and his gang are out of the picture but he had help. That message from Betsy Schultz was a warning."

Seamus Doherty feared that Nate Coppersmith would have stars in his eyes and not understand the danger. "There are killers waiting for us, Nate. We will have to fight them with our guns, our fists, and our brains. Outlaws are not brilliant geniuses, old man, and we have to go in with our eyes and minds wide open and awake."

Was Nate listening? Would he only see green grass and fat cows? Or was he mentally ready to fight for what was rightfully his? Seamus Doherty had spent so many years taking on gangs of ugly men out to steal anything they could, kill whenever they felt like it, and thumb their noses at the law. "It's the man with the brains who wins in fights like we're about to be in. We'll ride slow and cautious, Nate. Come in from some angle that wouldn't normally be used and know what we're riding into by observation. Are you with me?"

"I am, Seamus. I am," Coppersmith said. "I understand the danger; I'm ready to stand up to those yahoos, ready to kill to get back what is mine. I'm also anxious to see my ranch again, to smell the grass and hear the animals."

They rode quietly in the gathering twilight toward a rocky ridge about half a mile in front of them, absorbed in their own thoughts. Seamus fully aware they might be riding into a nest of killers who were probably expecting them. Coppersmith visualizing his ranch, his herd, seeing his children romping in the pastures, not fully aware of just what might be on the other side of the ridge.

It was an easy ride down the backside of the hill toward the home place. They were

riding at a slow walk on their approach, eyes darting side to side, ears all but pricked for the slightest sound. They saw the mostly dark ranch house and pulled their horses up short.

"Expected to find lights on," Seamus said, dismounting.

"Looks like just one small lamp lit in the kitchen," Nate said. "I don't see any other light, Seamus. Maybe no one's there."

"Don't bet on that. Let's tie these puppies off and take a nice slow walk up to that big house of yours. We'll go around the corrals there, through the brush keeping low, and should get darn close and out of the light. No moon, and that's on our side," he chuckled.

They rounded the corner of the corral that stood closest to the main house when a clatter of falling tin pans, buckets, and other metal objects came crashing down just a couple of yards in front of them. Doherty hit the ground fast pulling Coppersmith down with him and all but buried the two of them in surrounding brush.

I haven't pulled that kind of trick for years, Doherty

remembered. This is something Corcoran would do and that means he is expecting trouble. And that means me and old Nate here could be targets real soon.

"What the hell...," Coppersmith said before Doherty shushed him and the two, prone in the dirt, listened for anything.

"Be quiet, Nate. Someone set a trip wire and that means they know we're here. I just hope it was set by Corcoran and hope even more that he doesn't shoot us. Now, be quiet and we'll move very slow and very low to the ground."

"What the hell was that?" Betsy jumped from her chair and rushed to one of the new shooting ports in the bunkhouse.

"We have company, my dear," Corcoran said. He stood up and casually picked up his rifle, motioned to Dancing Antelope to follow, and moved toward the door. "Betsy, you get your rifle and cover us. Shoot the visitors, not us," and he gave her a quick kiss on the forehead and a gentle pat on her generous bottom.

"Well, now," she murmured, a little grin on her face, and stuck her rifle barrel out the shooting hole. "That was unexpected." She watched the two men duck out the door and make a dash across open ground, diving behind one of the large watering troughs near the corrals. There was no moon but the lingering effects of twilight offered some help.

Corcoran heard the barest of a scrape about twenty feet or so in front of him, motioned Dancing Antelope to circle around to his right, and he moved forward, ever so slowly on his belly, rifle at the ready. There, somebody twitched. They knew he was there and he knew where they were. There was enough light left that he could see the silhouette of brush, corral posts and, he thought, a man's body.

He caught a slight movement just to his left, brought his

Winchester up, and fired, jacking a second round quickly. He heard a howl instantly and held his fire. At the sound, Dancing Antelope rushed in and Corcoran did the same. Dancing Antelope was about to swing his rifle barrel down on a man's head when he stopped.

"Damn, damn, damn," he said. "Nate man, what you doing out here? Corcoran, it's Nate Coppersmith!"

There was a moan from under a large sage and Corcoran found Seamus Doherty nursing a serious wound to his arm. Corcoran grabbed him up and ran to the bunkhouse, yelling for Dancing Antelope and Coppersmith to follow. "Come on, Seamus, don't fight me, man. It's Terrence that's got you."

He put Doherty onto a cot and ripped the shirt from him, calling Betsy over. "Get some hot water and I'll get the bleeding stopped." He used the ripped shirt to wipe the wound area and then press the shirt into it. "Bullet went all the way through. Can you hear me, Seamus?"

"I can hear you. You're howling loud enough for folks in Oregon to hear you, Corcoran. How bad is it?"

"You're gonna be sore for a while but you'll live. Damn, man, why didn't you yell out who you were? I could have killed you. Can you move your arm? Did the bullet break your arm?" He couldn't stop talking as he watched Doherty flex his arm a bit, grunt from the effort, but smile just a little. It's one thing to shoot an outlaw, particularly one who wants to shoot you, but an entirely different matter when one shoots a dear friend.

"Not broken, Terrence. No bullet to worry about? Good. Patch me up and tell me what's going on. I'm not big on being shot, Corcoran, and particularly by men that I've befriended." The comment was offered with a wry grin but Corcoran understood that he'd best be on good behavior for a while.

It wasn't the first time Seamus Doherty had been shot in

his long career with Wells Fargo but it was the first time he'd been shot by a friend. Being shot angers a man but being shot by a friend, accidentally, leaves one unable to be angry, particularly when one knows he would have done exactly the same thing.

"Don't worry yourself about it, Terrence. It's just a good thing you can't shoot straight."

That brought chuckles from everyone except Corcoran who had enough sense to keep his mouth shut.

Corcoran spelled out what he and Dancing Antelope were planning and Betsy filled the newcomers in on what had taken place in the village. "It sure makes sense to me," Doherty said when she was through. "I've never met this Peabody character but I've heard many stories."

"How would Peabody know enough about what you were planning, Coppersmith, to get the word to Curly Joe Simpson?" Corcoran asked. He had a pot of coffee boiling on the little stove in the bunkhouse and Betsy had all the lamps lit.

"It's probably my own fault," Nate said. He was sitting on a bench along the front wall, holding his head in his hands. "I needed a full-time ranch foreman. Dancing Antelope was my first choice but he couldn't work full time. I needed to take Susan and the children to Winnemucca for the winter and spread the word far and wide looking for a foreman."

"I'm still concerned that the sheriff or that federal land agent is involved." Doherty was pacing around, poured some coffee and sat on one of the bed frames. "We better make sure we're ready for Peabody or his gang, Terrence. I destroyed your little noisemaker out there."

"It worked once, it'll work again," Corcoran said. He, Coppersmith, and Dancing Antelope headed out to rebuild the alarm system and Doherty stayed inside with Betsy, enjoying his coffee and nursing his wound.

"I saw the way you've been looking at that man, Betsy.

Fair warning, girl, he's not one to settle down yet. You may have him twisted around and not thinking clearly, but he'll bolt at the first opportunity."

"I'm sure you're right, Seamus. My dad said the same thing and I can see it in his eyes." She had different thoughts, though. *I'm gonna do what I can to end his venturing days. I want to wake up in the morning looking into those eyes.* "I'm not a naïve little girl. He thrives on danger and on helping people who need it the most. I'm aware, but I'm going to give him the biggest fight of his life."

"We can't defend this place at all," David Schultz said. He was pacing back and forth in the little office in Grant County, Oregon. There was a window on one side of the front wall and a door on the other but no other windows. The building was two stories high but was long and narrow. At the back of the lower floor, where the two cells were, there was a door that was barricaded with a simple plank laid across as a crossbar.

Most of the buildings in the little community were made of unpainted wood and in the high desert that wood dried quickly. Fire was responsible for more death and destruction on the frontier than any other cause except maybe winter flu. "If I was looking to spring Simpson, I'd use fire. Either burn the jail or start one somewhere else to draw us away. Let's move to the saloon. It'll be warmer and much safer."

Brownie went to the back and got Simpson in handcuffs and manacles, and they walked across the street to the Golden Gulch Saloon. Schultz walked in front with his rifle at the ready while Crazy Dog covered their backs, his rifle also ready. Simpson was limping and moaning as they crossed the street and Brownie nudged him hard twice to keep him moving.

"I left a lamp burning on the desk so if someone does show up, they'll think I'm in there," Schultz said.

"I wonder if this threat from Peabody is real?" Brownie thought he might have had his fill of excitement for the time being. "Just who is he, anyway?"

"He is bad man," Crazy Dog said. "He has bad men working for him. Army thinks he is trader but he is outlaw. I know. Shorty Crandall work for him and Shorty really bad man. Kill people just because. Kill my uncle one day because my uncle get in his way on road to Fort McDermott. Laughed when my aunt cried. Hope he comes here. I kill him."

Schultz knew then to take the warning that Betsy and the lieutenant had sent very seriously. "Let's keep the lamps here low and the fire hot. Brownie, you take the first watch. Use the front windows but don't make yourself a target. I would think if anyone's going to try to break Simpson out, they would hit the jail, not a saloon."

"Peabody won't be trying to break me out, Schultz. He wants me dead. That note you read is right. He was my partner." Simpson was still hurting from the beating he took but did get a slight chuckle out. "I'm not going down alone, Schultz. I'll tell you everything if you keep me alive."

"I'll do my best, Simpson, but the army's gonna hang your ass high when they get their hands on you. If someone does show up and you attempt to make a move or a sound, I'll shoot you dead. Got it?"

Simpson just snickered and settled deeper into his blanket near the big stove. "Keep me warm and safe, Sheriff."

The night was cold, there was no moon, and Crazy Dog relieved Brownie sometime around midnight. "Coffee's hot, Brown. Sheriff sleeping, Simpson snoring loud, and the fire is hot. I watch now."

"I haven't seen or heard a thing, Crazy Dog. Stay sharp," Brownie said.

After about two hours, Crazy Dog got up and stretched, walked over to the door and slowly opened it. The bitter cold night flowed around him and he welcomed it. He stepped out onto the street in time to see two men on foot, making their way toward the sheriff's building. He slipped back in and woke up the sheriff and Brownie.

"Two men working way toward jail. Go around in back. Brownie, you and me go around this side; Sheriff, you go other side. We catch 'em up."

"Best plan I've heard," Schultz said.

The three men eased out the saloon's doors, Brownie and Crazy Dog to the left and Schultz to the right. All three carried rifles and had their sidearms handy as well. The street was narrow and most of the buildings were separated by a few feet of open space. Trees were spread up and down the street and the men moved through the darkness quickly, ducking from tree to building to tree to get onto the street behind the jail building.

"Got here mighty fast," Schultz muttered. "Brownie never had a chance to find us help and we don't have time to try to wake anyone up around town. Play it out with the cards we have," he chuckled.

"You follow behind, Brown, but not too close," Crazy Dog said. He left his blanket in the saloon and, in moccasins, soft buckskin leggings and breechclout, and buckskin shirt, he moved quick and quiet through the cold darkness. He and Brownie edged down the street toward the back of the jail and saw two men piling brush and weeds around the base of the building.

"They're gonna burn it down," Brownie whispered.

Crazy Dog slipped behind a large cottonwood tree about a hundred feet or so from the men and raised his rifle. He looked over to Brownie and nodded. As they had discussed before leaving the saloon, Brownie said, "Hold it, you two.

This is Deputy Sheriff Brown speaking. Stop what you're doing."

Shorty Crandall dropped his torch, spun, drew his revolver just in time to catch a large chunk of lead from Crazy Dog's rifle. He dropped to the ground and tried to scramble behind some boxes piled up near the building. Floret tried to run away and rapid fire from the sheriff stopped him cold. Floret never got his weapon in hand.

"Give it up, Crandall," Crazy Dog yelled. "You hurt bad. You fight more, you gonna die slow, bad man."

His answer back was two quick shots that blew considerable bark from the cottonwood. "Oh, bad choice, Crandall. I kill you now." Crazy Dog was on his belly squirming through the dirt and mulch toward the building next to the jail, almost invisible in the darkness. Brownie took that opportunity to put a couple of shots toward Crandall to keep his head down.

Schultz moved closer to the jail from the other side trying his best to not be in the line of fire from Brownie and Crazy Dog. He was stretched out behind a fence post and one of Crandall's legs was visible. He pulled down with his Winchester and slowly squeezed the trigger. The blast from the shot was mixed with the yowl of pain from the outlaw and Schultz jumped up and ran to the writhing man.

"One little mistake, buster, and you're dead," he said, shoving the rifle barrel into Crandall's chest. Crazy Dog ran up, followed immediately by Brownie. "Check on the other one, Brownie. Make sure he's dead or unable to hurt anyone."

Floret was still breathing but there was a steady flow of blood from his chest and Brownie kicked his weapon aside. "He's alive, Sheriff, but not for long, I think."

"Let's see if we can get these men in the saloon. Brownie, if our gunshots haven't already wakened the town, why don't you knock on some doors and see if we can get some help? It would be really good if we can keep at least one of them alive."

"Why?" Crazy Dog was shaking his head in wonder. "Indian way is best. Kill your enemy. Now, you gonna take all the time to make them well, put them in building where man in black blanket say they die, and then kill them. Indian way is best."

Schultz had to laugh and was shaking his head as well. "You're probably a lot more right than any of us know, Crazy Dog, but it is our law and it is our way. See if you can drag that one you called Crandall over to the saloon and I'll get this one here. Yup, we'll keep 'em alive long enough for the government to kill 'em. There are times I wish I was an Indian."

CHAPTER NINETEEN

"How much farther, Peabody? Sun'll be up shortly. We should have been there two hours ago." Waco Bob Torrez didn't like Peabody's plan to begin with and moving slow all night brought him close to a rage. They had left the little village much later than Waco Bob would have and then traveled as if they were on a Sunday afternoon lark.

"The time to hit an enemy is two hours or so before sunrise, Henry. I told you that yesterday. We're still miles from that ranch and it's light enough to be seen. You need to ride with us once in a while when we do these jobs. You're getting soft."

"We're doing things my way," Peabody snarled. "I hired you, Waco Bob, and that means you work for me. Let's not forget little things like that." Peabody turned in the saddle to look at Waco Bob and wondered if maybe he should not have spoken so harshly. He forgot sometimes that the men he hired were killers and many didn't much care who the next victim might be.

Waco Bob stiffened visibly; the look on his face was hardened into a granite-like frown that would frighten most men into instant surrender. Peabody turned away from the scowl and put his horse into a gentle trot, leaving the outlaw two choices. Shoot his boss in the back or forget anything was said. For one of the few times in his life, Waco Bob swallowed his pride and nudged his horse a bit.

Jason Kimble had found two more men to ride with them and Peabody thought five guns would be more than enough. "Everything's gonna work out fine, Bob," Peabody said. "There are five of us and we're going up against an Indian and a wanna-be tough guy cowboy. How hard do you think this is gonna be? What's important is that I get there, take posses- sion with my signed bill of sale from Simpson, and then get word to Reg Chapman."

Waco Bob didn't say a word but the scowl never left his face either. He'd killed men for less than what was just said and Peabody said it in front of the others. It was like a slap in the face and nothing would anger a man to killing than an open-handed slap.

Anger at Simpson still boiled through Peabody's veins. Simpson was supposed to take legal possession of that ranch and immediately sell it to Peabody who in turn would sell it at a good price to anyone with cash in hand. Simpson played stupid, tried to take airs, strut around like a big old rancher, and destroyed the timing of the deal. Many thousands of dollars lost because of that.

They rode in silence until the sun was well into the sky before they dropped into the Pueblo Valley and saw the Sleepy U spread out across the desert. Instead of following the natural terrain into the valley, Waco Bob led them into draws and canyons, keeping the line of riders out of sight until they hit the valley floor.

"Best bet, Peabody, is to spread out, way out, and get as close as possible, then make the last several hundred yards on foot." Waco Bob was using a scope to look at the home ranch. "Ain't enough trees or brush to hide a horse. If we move in on the barn and corrals, we'll have a good shot at getting into the main house."

"That's a good plan, Bob," Peabody said. Waco Bob was one of the best at setting up an attack, whether it be a bank, a gold shipment, or a ranch. "Remember," Peabody continued, "let's do as little damage as we can to those buildings. Everybody gets a piece when we sell that place." Peabody was at the ranch once or twice after Simpson took it over and knew he would get a good price for the ranch, land, and cattle if it could withstand this attack.

"Jackson, you and Tall Tommy swing way out to the right and move in slow toward the back of that barn. Kimble, you and Peabody move off to the left there and come in behind what looks like a bunkhouse. I'll move down through the brush and work my way through those corrals. Everybody got that?" Waco Bob looked around the group and got nods.

"One thing," Peabody said. "Nobody makes a move to the main house until I say so. We'll use as little force as we have to. We're only looking at an Indian and a cowboy so this should be fairly easy."

Waco Bob just shook his head wondering where Peabody had been all these years.

There's nothing easy about raiding a ranch, a bank, a stagecoach, or a pigsty for that matter.

"Don't hesitate to kill anything that moves, gentlemen. This is not going to be easy." He glared at Peabody giving him a look that should have made the man back off but Peabody didn't recognize what was said in those fearsome eyes. "Those men will have rifles and pistols and if we surprise them, it'll be best. Go in as if they're not going to be surprised." The outlaw growled as he nudged his horse into a walk and his scowl was fierce if Peabody had looked.

Waco Bob waved the bunch off and watched them trail

down through a maze of drainage gulches toward the ranch. "Bill Jackson and Tall Tommy Thompson will do fine," he murmured to himself, watching the two ride off slowly. "Kimble's a good man but Peabody doesn't have any idea what we're doing. We should have been here at three this morning. Hell, we won't be at that damn barn before noon."

"You see that dust, Terrence?" Betsy was pointing toward a hillside about two miles to the north. They were bringing water and firewood into the bunkhouse. Most of the morning had been taken up with preparing for an assault and wondering why one hadn't already taken place.

"Been watchin' it. Let's get everybody together, Betsy. We're about to have more company." Corcoran and Betsy would defend the bunkhouse, Dancing Antelope would defend the barn and corrals, and Seamus and Nate would work from the main house. Corcoran had the group huddled in the dust along a corral fence, everybody watching the dust trails on the hillside.

"Looks like they've split up, Terrence," Seamus Doherty said.

"Yup. That makes sense. I count five of 'em. They'll come from the backside of the buildings, I'd wager, and those little traps we set this morning might just shake 'em up some. Let's do everything we can not to kill these yahoos. Nate, we want answers, not dead outlaws.

"Somebody besides Simpson, and I'm guessing Peabody like you said, Betsy, was behind all this. But there might also be someone behind Peabody so let's not kill everybody."

Corcoran waved them off to their positions and he and Betsy walked into the bunkhouse. "They'll come up from behind the building and there aren't any windows there which means they'll have to come around where we can see them."

He walked around the room trying to figure out the best places from which to watch.

"I think we'd be better off outside, pretty lady. Come on," and he headed for the door. They moved around behind the building and Corcoran spotted what looked like a pile of old equipment including harness, wagon parts, even junk wood and furniture. "There's our fort. Let's burrow down in that mess and we'll have a clear view if a couple of those jerks come down this way."

"You have one of your little traps right over there," she said. She was pointing at a group of cottonwood trees with a footpath through them that led to the bunkhouse. Back on the other side of the trees were the outhouses. "Be like a turkey shoot."

"Don't ever bet on something like that," he said. "If Dancing Antelope was right, these are hardened criminals, Betsy. They aren't gonna just walk in and give it up."

"I know," she said. "Remember who my dad is. But if they walk down that path and stumble on your surprise, they'll be sitting ducks." She had to chuckle at the picture she saw and Corcoran did, too.

They settled in for the long wait and kept their eyes on the well-worn footpath. Corcoran had a length of cord stretched tight between two trees at a narrow part of the pathway that, when pulled or jerked, would trip a platform of tin cans and junk high up in the trees. It would rain down on whoever tripped the cord, make a hell of a racket, and startle the outlaws for a moment or two.

"They won't come across from the corrals, Nate. They'll come at us from behind the house. Go upstairs and take a position by a window that gives you a good look at where they might come. I'll stay down here and use whatever windows I need.

Don't take any foolish chances, Nate. I know we want a prisoner, particularly Henry Peabody, but don't try to wound.
Shoot to kill. A wounded man can fight and shoot just as well
as one not wounded."

Nate Coppersmith was standing in his home and couldn't
move. All the furniture was still where he had last seen it,
pictures were hung, stuff was on tables, and memories
flooded his mind. He saw his children romping, saw Susan
sitting in her rocker sewing, could almost smell his pipe being
lit in the evening. I'm home. I'm really back in my home and,
by damn, I'm never leaving again. How could I have been so
stupid to let that man make a buffoon of me.

"Wake up, Nate." Seamus shook Copperfield out of his
reverie and the big man lumbered up the staircase to take a
position at an upper window. Seamus found a spot in the
living room where he could see out toward the rear of the
house and toward the barn and corrals. "Five of them and five
of us. Never had better odds in all my years," he chuckled. He
was also well aware that only he and Corcoran had ever been
in a gunfight with known killers. "I better add Dancing Antelope to that short list. Bet he's been in some pretty fierce
fights."

But would Nate Coppersmith hold up to it? He was big,
strong, defending his own property, but would he be able to
sight down that long barrel of a rifle and simply pull the
trigger to kill another man? What about Betsy Schultz? Sure,
her father was a sheriff, but had she even ever been in a fight
with another person? Could she shoot a man? These questions raged through Doherty's mind as he moved from
window to window, doing his best not to be seen and hoping
he would spot some movement before the shooting started.

Dancing Antelope walked into the barn, looked around, then

walked through and out the backside. There was a dirt and
dung heap off to the side a hundred feet or so and he walked
to it. It had been there long enough that sage and other brush
were growing in places. He made a nest under one of the
bushes and settled in for the siege that was coming his way.

Corrals spread around the far side of the barn from his
position and he and Corcoran had strung cord from one of
the corral corners to an upper level in the barn where a platform was filled with every kind of junk that would make
noise. The cord extended out several feet from the corral
fence and, if stumbled over, would trip that platform. "Hope
it scares them more than me," he joked when they put it
together. "That one that scared Nate made me jump, too."

Corcoran had chuckled remembering how he had jerked
about when all those cans and broken glass came tumbling
down. "Did this to some bank robbers once and scared the
posse more than the gang."

Bill Jackson and Tall Tommy Thompson rode as close to the
barn and corrals as they dared and tied off their horses.
"There's back doors to that barn, Tommy," Jackson said. "It
looks like they're open. If we go in that way, we'll have good
shots toward the big house. Gotta be .quiet though so we
don't spook the horses in the corrals. Probably some in the
barn, too."

Thompson stood almost six four and was rail thin. "We're
gonna have to crawl along the corral, Bill, and those horses
are already milling about some. They know we're here. Waco
Bob was right. We should be doing this in the dark. Sure as
hell somebody's gonna see us."

Jackson shushed him and they started crawling along a
fence line toward a corner where they could see into the barn.
"Probably nobody in there. Peabody said there was just an

Indian and a cowboy supposed to be here. When we get to that corner, cover me and I'll run to the side of the barn."

Thompson watched the horses in the corral milling around, worried some by two men crawling through the dust near them. "Nice and slow, Jackson. These horses don't much care for us being here."

The horses milling about kicked up a cloud of dust and Dancing Antelope immediately had two men picked out as targets. "Be fun when they hit that trip cord. Horses go crazy," he chuckled. Jackson was in the lead with Thompson about a yard behind him.

"See anything?" Thompson asked when Jackson stopped near the corner.

"No," Jackson answered. "Here goes," he said, standing at a stoop and taking the first step in his run for the barn. He immediately tripped on the cord and the platform high atop the barn was sprung loose.

It sounded like a falling cascade from hell; empty metal buckets, chunks of iron, tin, and copper crashed to the ground. Six big ranch horses in the nearest corral went nuts, screaming in terror, kicking, bucking, in a desperate attempt to flee whatever monster was out to eat them.

Jackson stopped dead in his tracks and was dead half a second later as a rifle was fired from the dung pile. Tall Tommy Thompson turned to flee and a second bark from that rifle tore half his head away. The clatter would have been heard across most of the home ranch area, the terrified horses made dreadful noises, but it was the two gunshots that were definitely heard.

"Sounds like trouble, Henry," Jason Kimble said. The two men were working through a stand of cottonwood trees, ready to make a move on the bunkhouse. "I know gunshots but what was that other noise?"

"Don't know," Peabody said. "Came from near the barn and only two shots. I'd say that whoever was there, Thompson and Jackson took care of the matter." It never occurred to him that the shots came from others, not his men. "Let's keep moving. Waco Bob is coming up toward the front of the ranch house so we need to clear out the bunkhouse if someone's there."

Kimble was staring at the bunkhouse and thought the best bet would be to run up to the back wall as quietly as he could. With no windows on that wall, it would be a fairly safe move. He crouched at the edge of the trees, looked back at Peabody, turned and made his sprint. He tripped the surprise which fell almost as a unit on Peabody's head, knocking the man out instantly.

Kimble found himself looking down the barrel of a Winchester held by a woman whose

hair literally sprung outward in every direction. "Make one little twitch, mister, and you're dead." Betsy motioned for him to drop his weapons and move toward the bunkhouse while Corcoran ran to where Peabody was spread out on the ground, covered in fifty pounds of debris.

Betsy was walking Kimble toward the bunkhouse wall and she thought he just might try to run, being taken by a woman and all. "You don't want to know how many men I've killed," she said quietly, nudging the outlaw in the back with the rifle barrel. "My daddy and I fought off the Bannock's and Shoshone more than once and they die hard. Move it," she said.

"That was fun to watch," Corcoran chuckled, getting Peabody on his feet. "Let's take these yahoos to the main house, Betsy. I think this old outlaw just wet himself." He waved over toward the barn and Dancing Antelope came out with a broad smile. "Looks like he got his man. Better get in the house quick. I counted five horsemen, we have two,

Dancing Antelope probably shot one, and that leaves two out there somewhere."

It was a quick dash across the barnyard, Betsy shoving Kimble ahead with that rifle and Corcoran almost carrying Peabody. Dancing Antelope was right behind, his rifle at the ready as they rushed through the kitchen door finding Doherty, rifle in hand, waiting for them. "Good job," he said.

Nate came downstairs and joined the group. "Is it over?" He had half a smile on his face, as if he could anticipate actually living on his own ranch again. "That's Peabody," he said, pointing at the man slumped in one of the chairs at the kitchen table. "Has he said anything?"

"Take it easy, Nate," Doherty said. "We're about to find out. Let's get a fire going in the stove, get some coffee on, and start being alert again. There are still outlaws out there. This isn't a game, damn it. Nate, get back on watch out the back of the house; somebody better keep an eye on this side."

Betsy made for the stove, Dancing Antelope was tying Kimble to one of the chairs while Corcoran tied Peabody up. Doherty moved a chair over to one of the kitchen windows and watched. "These two are who you captured, Terrence?" Corcoran nodded. "And you killed your man, Dancing Antelope?"

"Killed two mans," Dancing Antelope said. "Falling junk scared one into standing still and I put bullet right through his middle. Other man jumped to run and I killed him, too."

"That means we're missing one person," Corcoran said. "Think he'd stick around to try and save his boss?" He looked at Doherty who gave him a sarcastic look back. "Didn't think so. Let's not let our guard down, though. You just never know with outlaws what they might do. If they were smart to begin with, they wouldn't have to be outlaws."

Corcoran stepped back from Peabody, gave Betsy a big smile. "I'm gonna check on Nate. Why don't you come with

me, Dancing Antelope? Need to calm that big feller down."
They walked off toward the great room.

Betsy was tending the stove, had a big pot of coffee boiling. "I need a bucket of water," Betsy said. "I'll be right back," and she moved to the door.

CHAPTER TWENTY

Waco Bob was working slowly through scattered sagebrush and cedar, making his way toward the barnyard. "If it was three in the morning, I'd just walk right on in," he muttered, almost crawling through the dust and dirt. "When this is over, I'm gonna be moving on. Peabody's gonna get people killed the way he's been doing things."

He could see the dust being kicked up by the horses in the corrals. "Boys are moving through there too fast. Somebody's gonna see that." He was as startled as Jackson had been when the junk pile fell to the ground. That was followed by two quick rifle shots and Waco Bob knew that Jackson and Thompson were dead. He scrambled closer to the corrals, staying inside the line of brush and heard the second dramatic crash of garbage.

"What the hell is going on?" he mumbled. Within minutes he saw Corcoran and Betsy lead Peabody and Kimble out from behind the bunkhouse. They were joined by Dancing Antelope and everyone went into the main house. "So much for just a cowboy and an Indian. There were people in the big house, too. Damn you, Peabody."

His first reaction was to work his way back to his horse, mount that bucking monster, and flee to Colorado. Instead, he moved just slightly so he had a better view of the ranch house and decided to just lay in the dirt and watch for a while. "I might get something out of this yet," he said. "There are no less than four people that I've seen, and maybe more, so there is no hope of trying to rescue that fool Peabody. It's his stupidity that led to this but I might come out with something if I just watch for a short time."

Five minutes later, Betsy Schultz walked out the kitchen door with a large pail in her hand. A kitchen well was less than twenty feet from her, maybe a hundred feet from Waco Bob, and Bob started his approach, first to the side of the bunkhouse, then across the yard using a wagon and a cotton-wood tree for cover, and whacked Betsy across the side of the head, knocking her out cold.

Waco Bob Torres flung the woman over his shoulder and scampered back the way he had come, past the tree and wagon, around the bunkhouse and into the heavy brush. It took him ten minutes to work his way to his horse, jumped on with Betsy laid across the saddle, and rode slowly along the bottom of a ravine toward the rocky hills to his north.

"Wasn't what I came for," Waco Bob chuckled, "but it's not bad. I can have some fun tonight, hold her for ransom if I want, or just dump her and make for Denver. No more nonsense with Henry Peabody."

"Betsy went for water by herself?" Corcoran was ready to kill he was so angry. "You let her go by herself? Damn, Seamus, why?"

"She had her rifle, Terrence. If you're that worried, let's go help her with the water. She's strong and tough."

They grabbed rifles and headed out the kitchen door

toward the well. The bucket was alongside the rock frame-work, footprints from Betsy and one other were seen, and Corcoran hollered, "Find Dancing Antelope and have him follow me. You stay here with Coppersmith. No sumbitch is gonna hurt that girl while I'm alive." He took off at a dog-lope following a very evident trail.

I'm not gonna let anything happen to you, Betsy. Be as tough as everyone says you are cuz I'm comin'. Damn all of this. I'm comin', girl. His mind was floundering with terrible thoughts that included the most devastating loss he could have. *I've almost decided about getting out of this business, marrying that charming woman, settling down, and then something like this happens. I'm gonna chase down every sumbitch that breaks the law or hurts women. Damn 'em all.* He was racing through the brush following big boot prints in the soft dirt, cussing to himself, ready to slaughter anything that got in his way.

Within minutes he found where Waco Bob had his horse and ran hard back to the barn

to saddle Rube for the chase. Dancing Antelope joined him after he had already ridden off.

"Between the two of us, we'll track that fool," Corcoran said. Until he discovered Betsy missing, he wasn't fully aware just how much he wanted to be close to her. He was always attracted to women and them to him, but this was different somehow.

"He's not trying to hide anything, Dancing Antelope. He's riding straight for Oregon." Waco Bob had ridden over the rocky ridge and connected with the road that led to the village, then taken the north fork toward Oregon. "There's been no traffic on this road since we were here a few days ago."

"Makes for easy tracking, Corcoran. We ride fast, maybe catch him quick. Shaggy Hair is fighter, Corcoran. He won't enjoy what he caught," the Paiute laughed, pretending to

duck punches from someone. Corcoran had to chuckle at the
thought of Betsy beating the hell out of her abductor.

"Hope you're right," he murmured. "If she doesn't whip
his skinny butt, I'm sure gonna." They rode at a hard trot,
Dancing Antelope in the lead, bent low over his horse's
shoulder watching the tracks of Waco Bob's horse.

It was getting late in the day when Dancing Antelope
pulled his horse up short. "That outlaw's horse getting tired,
Corcoran. Him riding too hard, carrying big load. They stop
or horse stop pretty quick."

"There are some trees and a spring a couple of miles up
the road. Think that's where they'll stop? Betsy would
remember that, but would she tell that guy?"

"Shaggy Hair pretty smart. Might not say nothing," he
chuckled. Dancing Antelope put his horse in a gentle trot,
continuing the chase. "She not tell, they ride too hard until
horse quit, then we catch 'em. Maybe hour from now."

Corcoran had to chuckle at Dancing Antelope's optimism
and touched his spurs to Rube. They rode in silence for the
next half hour or so until Corcoran spotted a little dust out in
front of them.

"I don't think that's a dust devil kicking that up, Dancing
Antelope. That's being made by a horse or horses." The
Paiute nodded and they kicked their horses up a notch to
gain on the outlaw and his beautiful hostage. Anger was
seething in Corcoran. His blood was hot from the moment
Seamus Doherty told him Betsy went out to get water
without anyone going with her.

He could almost feel her arms around him, see her wild
shaggy hair blowing in the wind, and enjoying a long kiss
from her warm lips. Shake it off, big man, he thought,
watching the little wisps of dust as they got closer. We're
coming, Betsy. Damn, I've never felt this way. Doherty said I
should give up running all over hell and gone, chasing bad

men, and settle down. It wouldn't be hard with someone like
Betsy alongside. He had to chuckle at the thought. Sure,
Terrence. And then along comes a bad man and I'm off on
the chase. But it was something to think about. His anger
was still there but so were some fine thoughts about a
future.

"They're off the road, Corcoran. Looks like they're riding
to that spring. We tuck our horses in ravine where Chasing
Rabbits caught sage hen and sneak in after dark."

"Sounds good to me, old man." They got off the road and
moved slowly through heavy brush to a fairly deep ravine,
dropped into it and rode another half mile before stopping.
They unsaddled their mounts and tied them to some brush
where the grass was still green.

Dancing Antelope led the way up the side of the ravine
and slowly peeked over the top toward where he thought the
cottonwood trees and spring would be. Corcoran crawled up
alongside and spotted the fire. "About a hundred yards or so,"
he muttered. They slowly crawled through the desert sands
and dust using brush to hide their movement, and got closer
than Corcoran thought they should be. It was just getting
twilight and he could see Waco Bob and Betsy clearly.

"She's tied up and bleeding," he said. Waco Bob had built
a large fire, had a pot of coffee

boiling, and pulled something from his saddlebags before
settling down near the fire.

"Sumbitch's hurt her, Dancing Antelope, and he's gonna
pay for that." He was whispering and got a strong nod and
some words, probably Paiute cussing, in return.

"Quit yer damn crying, woman." Waco Bob was stirring the
fire. The coffee was boiling and he walked to his horse with a
cupful. "There's coffee and some food if you promise not to

try anything stupid," he sneered at her. She grimaced but nodded and he bent down to untie her.

He gave her the cup, offered a leering smile, and walked back to the fire to get himself a cup. Corcoran watched as Betsy took a quick sip of the hot coffee and started working her wrists and fingers, getting feeling back. "She's gonna attack that guy," he murmured, getting a nudge from Dancing Antelope telling him to be quiet. Well, she is, he thought and held back his chuckle.

Waco Bob had just one thing in mind and it was the one thing Corcoran was not going to allow, nor was Betsy. "What are you looking around for, woman? Ain't gonna be nobody comin' to get you. Only man gonna get you is me," he laughed. "Better get ready cuz I ain't had a pretty girl in a long time."

He walked to his horse and reached into the saddlebag for a flask of whiskey and came back to the fire. Betsy was standing near the fire, a fresh cup of boiling coffee in hand. "Have a drink with me and then we'll have some fun," he sneered. He opened the flask and poured his cup full, turned to Betsy to pour her some and got a face full of hot coffee.

He was yowling in pain and Betsy gave him a huge kick in the groin, knocking him backward. He tripped and fell into the fire, screamed from the burn, and rolled out writhing in pain, some of his clothing in flames. She took off at a run toward the horse, whipped the reins loose from a bush and jumped in the saddle. In less than five seconds, Waco Bob was out of the picture and Shaggy Hair was out of the camp. "Catch her," Corcoran said, leaping to his feet and racing to tackle Waco Bob who was trying to scramble to his feet.

Dancing Antelope ran hard back to the horses, mounted bareback, and was chasing Betsy in moments. Corcoran slammed into Waco Bob at a dead run, driving the already injured man to the ground. He pounded his fist into the burned face of the outlaw four or five times, jumped off the man and stood over him, his big Colt in hand. He wanted to pull that trigger, almost did, but caught himself in time.

"Get up." Corcoran snarled, kicking dirt in Waco Bob's face. He reached down and pulled the man's pistol, got him to his feet and walked him to where Betsy had been tied, using those ropes to tie the man tight. "How's that feel, big man? You got your ugly face burned by Shaggy Hair, buster, and when she gets back I'm gonna give her all the rein she needs to whup your ass good.

"What's your name?" He got nothing back, just an ugly scowl. "Okay, that's fine with me. I'll just call you 'Ass'. How's that sound, Ass?" Waco Bob Torres didn't make a sound except for the little cries of pain from the scalding coffee, swift kick, and rolling about in the fire. Corcoran was shaking his head and smiling, understanding that everything that had been said about Betsy being one tough woman was true.

We won't need to hire anyone to work our ranch; she's worth two good hands by herself, he laughed right out loud at the thought.

Corcoran laid more wood on the fire, found the cup Betsy had and filled it with coffee. He spotted the flask and took a goodly swig of rotgut whiskey and grinned at Waco Bob. "Sorry, but there ain't enough left to share," and he took another swig.

It was more than an hour later that Dancing Antelope and Betsy Schultz came riding into camp. "She good rider but horse not very good. Caught her for you, Corcoran." She didn't wait for Dancing Antelope, just jumped from her horse and ran to the big man, flinging herself at him, almost knocking the two of them to the ground, splashing coffee everywhere.

"Nice to see you, too," he laughed. He held her tight, rubbed her back, and let her hang on as long as she wanted. "I had a nice chat with that fool over there, Betsy, and told him you might have a few things to say to him, if you like. Seems like he's just another dumb outlaw. He thought you might be good for a ransom. I told him I wasn't too sure of that."

He had to duck a quick wild right that almost caught him on the side of the head. The two of them were laughing as he danced away from a couple more wild swings, then they went into another embrace, clinging tight to each other. "I would have fileted that man and hung his meat from these trees if he'd hurt you."

Dancing Antelope suggested they leave at first light for the ride back to the ranch.

"Gonna be a cold night. Outlaw have bedroll, so Shaggy Hair have blanket. I have blanket but you don't, Corcoran."

"But, as you said, my Paiute friend, Betsy has blanket."

CHAPTER TWENTY-ONE

It was a slow ride back to the ranch. Waco Bob was tied to his horse that was led by Dancing Antelope and Betsy rode behind Corcoran who spent most of the ride telling stories of his days in Virginia City, his exploits riding messenger for a stage company, and of some of the mountain ranges he loved so much.

Betsy wondered if the man just might be ready to settle down. She could see a ranch house with a large rock fireplace and the two of them sitting near it. Would Corcoran recite poetry or sing to her with that deep melodic voice of his? Would their children have his beautiful hair or would they be faced with the shaggy mess she carried around?

He had his thoughts and she had hers, and the miles drifted by until they topped that rocky ridge and dropped down to the Sleepy U ranch, back into reality. Dancing Antelope led the group right up to the hitching rails just off the kitchen porch.

"I'm glad you're all back safe," Doherty said when they rode into the barnyard. He was looking at the bruised and burned face of Waco Bob. "He looks like he didn't want to

come back with you." Besides blisters from the boiling
coffee, Waco Bob's face was covered in bruises and cuts
from the thrashing by Corcoran; blood had dried and his
face was also streaked with black from the fire. Doherty
jerked him off the horse and let him fall face first to the
ground. "Found out some interesting news while you
were gone."

"I'll take care of the horses," Dancing Antelope said. The
group marched Waco Bob into the main house where Nate
Coppersmith was watching Peabody and Kimble. The two
outlaws were tied to chairs at the big table. Waco Bob Torres'
hands were tied behind his back and he was slammed into a
chair and tied off.

Waco Bob was glaring at Peabody. "I should have killed
you back on the trail, Peabody."

"Shut up," Doherty said, slapping Torres hard. "Mr.
Peabody has been nice enough to tell me a few things about
this arrangement he had with Curly Joe Simpson. Seems you
were right, Corcoran. Simpson and Peabody did have a third
partner. Want to make a wild guess who that might be?"

"Most people would say it was Sheriff Peters," Corcoran
said with a slight grin. "I don't think so, though. Peters had a
hate for Nate," he said, glancing at Coppersmith. "But I don't
think it would extend to his wife and children. My guess is
what I've thought all along, the land agent. Chapman was
always a slimy bastard in my mind and wouldn't give a damn
about wives and children, only about how much money he
could make."

"There you go, Terrence. Greed. It's always the money,
isn't it? Did you recognize this guy?" Seamus was pointing at
Waco Bob.

"I think I've seen his portrait on a flyer or two but don't
recognize him. I asked him what his name was and he
wouldn't tell me. I now call him 'Ass' and he seems okay with

that." Corcoran had to chuckle at his little joke and just got a scowl back from Seamus Doherty.

"Name's Robert Torres. They call him Waco Bob. Wanted in four states that I know of and some goodly rewards on the line, too."

"Well, then, Betsy Schultz, looks like you picked the right man to fling coffee at." Corcoran looked at her, then Doherty. "She caught him, I didn't, and neither did Dancing Antelope. She did." He walked around the table and put his arms around the girl. "This here little charmer busted this mean old outlaw into the dirt and dust of Nevada. She's the toughest of the bunch of us."

Betsy was scarlet by the time he finished but didn't try to wiggle free of his embrace. She wanted to tell the man right out that she loved him, but didn't. But she surely did love the big jerk.

Corcoran poured himself another cup of coffee, laced it with some of Coppersmith's good whiskey, and paced around the kitchen. "We're gonna have to be cautious, Seamus. This isn't the time to go forward like a mad bull chasing a herd of fresh heifers. With Sheriff Peters and Rocky Rockefeller in custody at Fort McDermott, and Curly Joe wrapped up with Sheriff Schultz, Chapman must be aware that he's next in somebody's sights."

"I agree. Let's step into the great room, Terrence. For just a minute." Corcoran gave him a questioning look but followed the former Wells Fargo detective in. They stood next to the fireplace. "I didn't want to say this in front of Peabody. Peabody told me that he has a bill of sale for this ranch issued by Curly Joe. If what Chapman did as far as paperwork goes, converting Coppersmith's claim to Curly Joe, and Simpson gave Peabody a bill of sale, Nate might have a hard time getting this ranch back in his name." Seamus had that look, Corcoran thought; that look of a defeated man.

"Maybe, maybe not," Corcoran said. "Have you seen this bill of sale?"

"The fool flashed it in front of Nate. I thought Nate would kill him but he held his temper. More than I would have, I think."

"Well, okay then. Would you follow my lead when we go back into the kitchen? Just go along with me on this?"

"Sure, and you know I will, Terrence. Want to tell me about it first?"

"Nope."

Sam Messing was sitting at his desk when Reginald Chapman came blustering in. It was a cold morning with the wind whipping through the streets of Winnemucca and the diminutive Chapman was wrapped in an old blanket coat that was so oversized it dragged on the ground.

"I have need of some information I believe you have, Acting Sheriff," he said in his most pompous way. "If what I've heard is true, I will also have need of your services."

"What do you want, Chapman?" Messing was still uncertain of his status, not fully aware of what had happened to Coppersmith, and didn't like the little officious land agent in the first place.

"I believe there may be an attempt to commit fraud, sir. Joseph Simpson has been taken into custody by an Oregon sheriff, and Nathaniel Coppersmith may be attempting to reclaim his ranch which was legally claimed by Mr. Simpson."

"What makes you think that, Chapman?" Messing thought that what the little man was saying should be said in front of a judge not a lawman. "You can prove those allegations? Seems like you should be talking to an attorney."

"I have certain information," he said. His little pointed nose was aimed at the ceiling, his beady eyes were narrowed, and there was the slightest grin on his face. "Well, are you going to do something?"

"Show me something that would make me do something. Anyone can spout off, Chapman, but I can't investigate what you've said without some kind of proof or information that could be brought to a court. It sounds to me like you're talking through your hat."

"How dare you," he stammered. "I'm the federal land agent. I'm accusing a man of fraud. It's your responsibility to arrest Nathaniel Coppersmith." He was ramrod straight, all five feet and six inches of him; his little pencil moustache would have bristled if there had been enough of it. "Do your duty, sir."

"I know my duty, Chapman, far more than you do." Messing started to rise from his desk, which frightened Chapman enough for the little man to back up a step. "You bring me proof and I'll follow through. You charge into my office and yammer at me and I'll throw your skinny ass into the Humboldt River. Bring me some kind of documentation, Chapman. Otherwise, get the hell out of my office." He was still on his feet, leaning forward with both hands on the desk. Chapman had backed all the way across the room and had his back to the wall.

"The county commission will hear about this, Acting Sheriff. You won't be acting when I get through with you." He tried his best to wave a finger back and forth at Messing.

Messing stood straight up, shoved his chair out of the way, took two big steps around his imposing desk and had to laugh as he watched Reginald Chapman make a dash for the doorway "You're welcome here anytime, Chapman, that you have documentation. Watch your step there," he said, laughing loud and hard, watching the little man scurry down the courthouse steps.

"Damn fool probably helped Simpson steal that ranch in

the first place." He sat down at his desk and continued that train of thought. "With Simpson in custody, there's no one watching that place. I better take a little ride out there and make sure everything's where it's supposed to be. Old Nate doesn't deserve any of this. Peters should have put a stop to it right away."

He didn't let his mind go any further than that; didn't wonder if Peters had anything to do with the fraud. Didn't wonder why Chapman was so incensed about something. Didn't question anything that seemed so out of place. Worried though about the condition of the ranch. "If I leave now, I can be at the ranch tomorrow. Then take a couple of days to see Captain Watson at Fort McDermott. I'm not sure I want to be sheriff."

"I'll have that man behind bars if it's the last thing I ever do." Reginald Chapman was, after all, a federal officer. A land agent. If he said something was wrong, then by damn it was wrong. "I'll just ride out to the ranch. With Simpson in jail, I'm sure that Peabody has already taken possession of the property. Why did Simpson take so long to arrange for the sale? That should have been done immediately."

Chapman paced around his office for several minutes, working out how best to get everything back to where it should be. "I'll pack up and ride to the ranch. If I leave in the morning, I can be there day after tomorrow." For the first time since he heard about Simpson being arrested, the little man almost smiled.

He left an hour or so after sunrise for the two-day drive. Unlike Messing, he was in a buggy drawn by a fine pacer, his gear just behind the seat. While Messing made the ride to the ranch cross-country, Chapman favored following known roadways. Messing was at the ranch the following morning and Chapman was a full day behind him.

"Lieutenant Buckmaster, it's good to see you back, sir." Sergeant Banion took the reins from the lathered pony as the lieutenant stepped off. "How are things at Fort McDermott?"

"Just fine, Sergeant. Put together a patrol for me, will you? Captain Watson has given us a small job to do. I want to pull out of here at sunrise. You and two men. We won't need a tracker." Banion hurried off with the commander's horse and Buckmaster slipped into his CP tent.

He sat at his desk and pulled his orders out to read them again, remembering that last interview with Captain Watson and the outlaw Rockefeller. "Captain Watson does have a way about him." He could still picture it:

Captain Watson had Rocky brought to his office. "They call you Rocky Rockefeller," he said. "I call you a dead man. Who besides Curly Joe Simpson was in on this plot to take another man's homestead?" Rockefeller stood silent, wouldn't even look at the captain.

Watson stood up, walked to the large and very ignorant outlaw, and slugged him square between the eyes. The manacled outlaw was kept on his feet by the guard holding him and the captain whacked him again, breaking the man's nose.

"Now, you miserable rat, tell me what I want to know." He drew his fist back and just like Peabody said to his gang, the outlaw started talking. Rockefeller spilled the entire plot to steal the ranch and sell it off quick for the cheapest of prices to his partner who would then sell it for a very high price. He gave out names faster than Watson could write them down.

Buckmaster had many thoughts as he contemplated his journey to the Sleepy U ranch in the morning. Putting outlaws in chains was always a pleasure but he knew that Betsy Schultz might still be at the ranch. That's where she was heading the last time he saw her and he most certainly wanted to see her again.

Sunrise found Sergeant Banion and two men mounted and ready when Buckmaster joined the patrol. "Ride with me, Sergeant, and I'll make you fully aware of what our mission is." He looked at the two soldiers, raised his hand and gave the forward ho signal. "There might be some shooting, and maybe not. What we will be doing is making right something that was very wrong, Sergeant. A man's ranch was ripped from him by some nasty people and we're going to see to it that he gets it back."

The ride to the Sleepy U was about a three-hour event and half an hour out, they passed a gentleman in a buggy who seemed to be out for an early morning ride. They didn't stop, just nodded, getting a scowl back because of all the dust. It was a cold but pleasant morning for the ride.

CHAPTER TWENTY-TWO

Corcoran and Doherty walked back into the kitchen and told the captives to stand along the wall nearest the stove. "Gentlemen, you are all going to be charged with crimes that will lead to a hangman's noose. People have died because of you and some have lost major life possessions. I won't take the least bit of crap from any of you." Corcoran paced back and forth along the line of outlaws, his hands comfortably holding a Winchester rifle. The men could easily see the hammer cocked and ready.

He motioned for Jason Kimble to step forward, turn around, and spread his legs. Corcoran stepped up behind the man and touched the barrel of his Winchester to the back of the man's head. The tension was palpable and flowed as a strong current through every person in the kitchen. Would Terrence Corcoran shoot an unarmed man?

"Seamus, would you be kind enough to empty this man's pockets? We know he doesn't have any weapons but I want to see everything he's carrying." Doherty did as he was asked, with Dancing Antelope, Betsy, and Nate sitting at the table watching the show. Betsy caught Corcoran's eye and he gave her just the slightest wink which brought a smile to her face. She and he were the only ones in the room that knew he was not going to kill the man.

Doherty put Kimble's few things on the table. Corcoran then had Waco Bob and Henry Peabody searched and their possessions piled on the table. "That's everything they have?" he asked Seamus.

"Seems like it."

"Good. Now, take them into the great room and put them on the large sofa, tied together so that if one moves, they all must move. Nate, you and Betsy help him. Dancing Antelope, I think we need another couple of buckets of water, if you could, please?"

Seamus thought he saw what was going on and got the outlaws moving, nodding to Betsy and Nate to follow. He was smiling just a bit as he gave a last look toward Corcoran. Corcoran just grinned like a little boy playing in the mud and walked toward the stove for a cup of coffee. "Guess I better stir up the fire some."

"Company coming, Corcoran," Dancing Antelope said, coming in with a bucket of water. They grabbed rifles and stepped out onto the kitchen porch, watching a single rider come into the barnyard. Doherty came out onto the porch just as the man reined up at the hitching rack.

"Sam Messing," Doherty said. "What brings you out here?"

"Glad you're here, Doherty. I don't know any of the particulars of what's going on with Nate Coppersmith, Reg Chapman, and this ranch, but something is and I wanted to make sure the ranch itself was still in good order." He nodded to Dancing Antelope and glared in Corcoran's direction, wondering who the big cowboy was.

"It is, Sam. I guess you're the sheriff now so you need to know everything. Say hello to Terrence Corcoran. If Nate gets this ranch back, it will be because of what Corcoran's been doing. Come on in and we'll talk some. Have a good ride?"

"Long and cold. Corcoran, eh? Heard of you," he said, sticking his grubby hand out for a shake. There was no smile on his face as he sized the man up.

"Hope you're nothing like Peters," Corcoran said. They shook and each gave the other a full look-see. Corcoran had been carrying a badge for a long time, was proud of the work he did, and felt only hateful anger toward lawmen who turned the corner. He wanted to shoot the former sheriff and wondered how this acting sheriff was going to do.

"Ain't nothin' like that fool."

It took a full pot of coffee, most of a bottle of fine bourbon, and half a dozen cigars and Messing was brought up to date, his eyes so wide Betsy thought they might pop right out of his head.

"That's the most amazing story I've ever heard," Messing said. "A plot to steal a man's ranch and sell it. I've never heard of such a thing. Nate, please understand that I was not involved in any of this. Damn that Peters. He should have stopped this right from the start." He had heard part of the story when he was with Peters at Fort McDermott. He remembered the captain saying the outlaws should have been arrested but he did not know any of the details.

"Now I know why Captain Watson was in such a fury. I thought the man would shoot old Peters right on the spot. What can I do? Chapman is head of all this homestead business as federal land agent. Isn't his word final?"

"Not in the case of fraud, it ain't." Corcoran and Messing started out questioning just what each stood for but after the long discussion, both felt comfortable. "I think any judge would understand how this little conspiracy was to work out." Corcoran had the hint of a smile and continued with his little talk. "I don't think you can simply sell a homestead claim until after the claim is patented. But if a claim is vacated, someone else can lay claim to it.

"What I see as fraud is Simpson claiming Nate's vacating, then vacating himself with a written document, not a bill of sale, allowing Peabody to lay claim. Peabody would then do the same for a big amount of cash and that person would have a homestead claim to fulfill.

"Complicated as all get out and that's what ruined the plan. Simpson is just too ignorant to have participated. I'm still putting my money on Chapman being behind the entire deal." Messing sat down at the table following Corcoran's description of the land deal shaking his head, almost in disbelief.

"We'll bring these yahoos into Winnemucca as soon as you arrest them on so many different charges and let the courts take it from there," Corcoran said.

"Nate should be named caretaker of the ranch until the final court decision. Then he and Susan can move back out here, the kids can romp on their own ranch, and I can go back to being a Eureka County Deputy Sheriff."

"Sounds like you think this is all wrapped up, Corcoran. I hope you're right," Nate said and was echoed by the rest of the table. Nate had held his anger in check for most of this horrible ordeal but Doherty could see it wouldn't take much for the man to fly into a rage. As big and strong as Coppersmith was, he could inflict some serious damage.

"The sooner that bastard Chapman gets arrested the sooner I get what's mine." He was shaking in his anger and frustration. "Is there anything short of taking a man's life worse than taking a man's ranch and home? Rustling cattle, stealing a horse is a hanging offense in most areas and stealing a man's ranch should be. Chapman is the foulest person I've ever met and I would gladly shoot that man dead." Coppersmith's rage was more than evident to everyone. "When can we leave for Winnemucca?"

"It's too late to start today so let's have a good supper, a quiet and comfortable sleep, and leave out of here first thing tomorrow," Doherty said. "That okay with you, Messing?"

"That should work. I need to figure out all these charges and formally arrest those men you have tied up. Somebody needs to stay at the ranch. Chapman was riled when he left my office and you can bet he'll attempt something."

"I stay." Dancing Antelope walked around the table and stood next to Nate Coppersmith. "I'm ranch foreman. My responsibility." End of question if anyone thought of suggesting otherwise. "Let's eat."

"For tonight, we need to separate the prisoners. We don't want them able to help each other get untied. Bind them up to something solid so they can't get to each other," Doherty said. "I remember having to bring three men in once by myself and it almost went to hell on me when one of them was able to help one of the others get free."

"Take 'em to the barn and hang 'em," Dancing Antelope said and Betsy gave a whoop in favor. Calmer heads prevailed, though.

Sunrise found the kitchen at the Sleepy U ranch as busy as if it were branding time. Betsy had the wood stove fired up and coffee made. She was busy frying great slabs of bacon along with potatoes and onions while Sam Messing and Terrence Corcoran were getting the prisoners up and ready to start the ride back to Winnemucca.

Doherty, Nate, and Dancing Antelope were packing two mules and catching up the horses to saddle them. "This'll be an impressive caravan when we ride into town, Nate. When we get these yahoos safely tucked behind bars, you go get

Susan and the kids. Corcoran, Messing, and I will round up Mr. Chapman and place his butt under arrest."

"I'd like to be with you when that happens, Seamus. I'm still worried this isn't going to work like you think it will. But I'd be mighty pleased if I could be with you when you arrest that rat."

Doherty remembered Nate's words the day before. Would Nate kill him on sight? Is that why he wants to be with the group when he's found? "No, Nate. It's best that you get Susan and the children out here as soon as possible." Nate nodded but his eyes said he didn't agree with Doherty.

It took far more time than anyone thought to get everyone fed and all the animals ready for the start to town. The prisoners were in the saddle and tied to their mounts, the horses tied as pack animals, the pack animals tied off and ready when Dancing Antelope announced a visitor approaching.

"Getting' to be like the emigrant trail," Corcoran joked. They watched four riders come in at a walk.

Corcoran and Messing strode out of the barn, rifles at the ready, to find Lieutenant Buckmaster and three soldiers riding in. "Well, looky here," Corcoran said. "Out on morning patrol, Buckmaster?"

"Looks like I got here just in time. Corcoran, we need to talk and I mean right now. Let's sit at the table." Corcoran noticed that Buckmaster was a different man than the one initially in on the chase for Simpson. Now, acting under direct orders of the post commander, he really was an officer in the U.S. Cavalry.

"Is this official type talk? Cuz if it is, we'll need Sam Messing at the table as well. He's the acting sheriff in the county now."

"Who are these men tied together?"

"I think you know Henry Peabody. The other two are

what's left of his gang. That's Waco Bob Torres and the other is Jason Kimble. There are warrants on both."

"Well, better get 'em off the horses and into the house. This might take a while to get done. I'm acting on direct orders from Captain Watson at Fort McDermott." The lieutenant told Sergeant Banion to get the prisoners off the horses and herded into the big house and to guard them carefully. "These men are known killers, Sergeant. Don't take any nonsense from them."

"We're not gonna have another set-to on jurisdiction are we?"

"Looks like it." Buckmaster smiled slightly. "Hello, Miss Schultz. Certainly nice to see you again." He bowed just a bit and offered his hand which she took and quickly let go.

The group was back seated around the kitchen table and, between Buckmaster and Corcoran, they spent almost an hour discussing the situation. "So," Corcoran said. "Rockefeller confessed to Watson that Simpson's partners were Chapman and Peabody. And Peabody confessed to us that Simpson and Chapman were his. What we need now is Chapman to be taken into custody. That's your first job when we get back to Winnemucca, Sam Messing, Acting Sheriff." He couldn't control the chuckle and Messing grinned along with him.

"That will be my pleasure."

"I just hope all this holds up in court," Nate Coppersmith said. Everyone in the room nodded in agreement. Corcoran and Messing had both faced messy trials in the past and knew there was no such thing as a guaranteed win in a court case. "I've just spent a day back in my home, slept in my own bed last night," he said. His voice was quiet, soft, and in many men that was a sign of building rage; be careful when an adversary began speaking and acting quietly.

"I will not lose this place again," Coppersmith said. His

long face was so sad and so filled with anger that Betsy got up and walked around the table to put an arm around the big man. He looked up at her, could just barely get a slight smile going. "I won't let this place belong to anyone else. Ever. What these men did is no less than taking a man's life. They should all hang and I'll be glad to help. Chapman should be first in line."

"Looks like more dust on the trail, Corcoran." Seamus Doherty stepped out on the kitchen porch, rifle in hand. "Looks like a buggy coming in. Somebody has one fine pacer out for a ride. Damn, that's a horse any man would want. You've seen that team that Meagan and I love to ride behind, Nate."

Reginald Chapman, his lips pressed in continued anger, drove his fine pacer into the barnyard and too late recognized Sam Messing and Seamus Doherty walking toward him, rifles pointed at his head. "What's the meaning of this?"

Dancing Antelope ran forward and caught up the pacer, calming the big gelding down while Corcoran yanked Chapman from the buggy. "Welcome to the Sleepy U, Mr. outlaw land agent. Sheriff Messing, if you please?"

Corcoran wanted to chuckle at his little comment but held it in long enough for Sam Messing to place Chapman under arrest. Nate Coppersmith came barreling out the kitchen door as they walked toward the house and tackled Chapman, driving the diminutive land agent into the dirt. He was about to punch him in the face when Corcoran pulled the beefy rancher off.

"I'd surely like to let you continue your actions, Copper-smith, but I can't. Hang on, old man, and all this will work itself out. Come on now, let's get some coffee and settle down some."

Coppersmith fought Corcoran to get loose and the two tussled for a couple of minutes before Corcoran finally got the big man settled down some. "Don't make this any worse than it is, Nate. You're the victim. Don't make Chapman a victim, too. Let the law take care of this."

"I want that man dead, Corcoran. I want my ranch back and I want these bastards dead." He was howling his anger and hurt to wide skies of the Great Basin, his eyes wet with tears, the anger held back for so long, it was splashed clearly across his face. Doherty slipped an arm around Nate's shoulder and nudged him back toward the kitchen porch and into the house where Betsy eased him down at the big table.

Buckmaster had the outlaws lined up, still tied together. Chapman was in handcuffs but not tied to the others. "I'm going to ask a few questions and I won't tolerate anything but the truth. Whose idea was this in the first place, this attempted land fraud?"

"There's no fraud," Chapman snapped. "Coppersmith abandoned his claim and Mr. Simpson filed properly."

"Lies," Coppersmith howled from inside the house.

Peabody said quickly, "That's the truth, Buckmaster. What Agent Chapman said is the truth, and Simpson sold that homestead claim to me. I'm now the legal owner of this ranch, pending the filing of all the paperwork."

The group was herded into the kitchen and lined up against the far wall. Buckmaster hadn't heard anything of Peabody buying the ranch; nothing had been said at Fort McDermott about it. He looked around the table. Doherty, Corcoran, and Messing just hunched their shoulders as if it was all new to them as well.

"Liar," Coppersmith yelled again. Corcoran stepped toward Nate just in case he went after Peabody again.

"That's quite a statement, Mr. Peabody." Buckmaster looked around at the outlaws and those standing about. "I don't believe Mr. Rockefeller said anything about that to Captain Watson. His comments were that you, Simpson, and

Mr. Chapman here were conspiring to steal this ranch. Do you have any proof of ownership? A bill of sale? A promissory note?"

"Indeed I do," Peabody said. "That pile of stuff on the table is our personal possessions that were taken from us. You'll find a bill of sale from Simpson to me, written, dated, and signed."

Buckmaster worked his way through coins, cash, leather pouches, tobacco and papers,

even a little sewing kit. It took several minutes as Buckmaster went back through the pile again. "I don't find anything of the sort here, Mr. Peabody. You're just wasting our time with this kind of nonsense."

"They took it from me," Peabody screamed. "It was there." Sergeant Banion smacked Peabody across the side of the head when he lurched forward, trying to drag the other prisoners with him.

"Is this everything you took from these men?" Buckmaster asked Messing.

"Everything's right there, Lieutenant. Nothing's been moved since we took the stuff from them. I never saw anything that looked like a bill of sale. Did you, Corcoran?"

"Nope. Just threw it all on the table there. He's lying just like Chapman is."

"Captain Watson is holding Rockefeller on charges of land fraud, which are federal charges. He has authorized me to arrest Peabody and Chapman on those same charges. What about these other men?"

"I don't think anyone is going to argue jurisdiction with you on this one, Buckmaster," Corcoran said. "According to Peabody, there might even be more members of his gang heading toward Oregon to do mischief. Remember, Lieutenant, Simpson is being held by the Grant County, Oregon sheriff. Peabody may have sent gunmen up there to set him free or maybe kill him."

"I'll send a patrol to Grant County first thing," Buckmaster said. "Now, what about these other men?"

"Attempted assault, assault with intent, and other local charges," Messing said. "What about Coppersmith's ranch? This needs to be addressed soonest. His family is in Winnemucca and should be out here."

"Captain Watson believes that Mr. Coppersmith can bring his family back and live here until the federal court works its way through this whole land fraud problem. In his opinion, the ranch is yours again, Coppersmith."

Nate let out a howl that would have put a Comanche to shame. He jumped from his chair and danced around the kitchen. There was bedlam for some time, with Peabody screaming that he had a bill of sale, Chapman screaming that he was a federal officer and demanding to be turned loose, while Corcoran sat at the table flirting with Betsy Schultz.

"We've managed to use up the better part of this day," Corcoran said as things calmed down. "What are your plans, Buckmaster?"

"I'll take Peabody and Chapman back to Fort McDermott to stand trial with Rockefeller and former Sheriff Peters, although there is no direct evidence that he was involved in the fraud. He enabled the fraud, these other men acted on the fraud.

"This Waco Bob fool and Jason Kimble are your prisoners as far as the army is concerned, Sheriff Messing. We'll be leaving within the hour. Captain Watson has instructed me to inform you, Corcoran, Mr. Doherty, Mr. Coppersmith, and Miss Schultz, to make yourselves available for the trial. You will be notified of the time and place."

"I just hope it's sooner than later," Nate said. "I want to see those men shackled and led off to prison where they can rot with their own kind. I want to be there when they hang and die."

Buckmaster led his patrol out of the yard, watched closely by Coppersmith. "Make you feel good, Nate?" Seamus Doherty was standing alongside the big rancher. "It's been a hell of an ordeal for you and the family. It's almost over now."

"Thank you, Seamus. Where's that big old Irisher? I gotta give him a hug and back pounding hard enough to cause bruises. What a mess." They stood in the late afternoon light watching the patrol until it disappeared over the rocky ridge to the north.

"We could leave out now and make camp in just a few hours or wait for first light and head for Winnemucca." Sam Messing was pacing around the great room, his two prisoners bound together on the sofa in front of the fire. "What's your preference, Corcoran?"

"If we didn't have them two, I'd leave out right now but tomorrow's first light would be better. Nate, what's your plan?"

"Gonna ride back with you folks and get my family."

"I want to ride in with you, too," Betsy said. "Susan is going to need a lot of help getting packed up for the trip back. She'll be so happy." She looked over to Corcoran and gave him a nice smile.

"I'm gonna check the horses and mules one more time," Corcoran said, draining his coffee cup.

"I'll join you," Betsy said. "I need a breath of fresh air. This has been quite a day."

CHAPTER TWENTY-THREE

"You still have a set of handcuffs with you, Messing?" Corcoran was riding alongside the new Humboldt County sheriff, the rest of the group trailed out behind. "When I got those yahoos up this morning, it looked a lot like Waco Bob had almost got himself untied. He's a slippery one."

"I'm glad you said something. I got mine back from that soldier boy so I have just the one set. We can cuff the two together tonight in camp."

They rode across a low set of hills and dropped toward the Queen's River, often called Quinn's River, and worked their way south. With six people and their horses and two pack mules, it was going to be a long slow ride back to Winnemucca. "I'm not worried about that Kimble feller. He might be big and strong but he's not anywhere near the danger that Waco Bob is."

"I agree with that," Messing said. "I've seen papers on Waco Bob Torres for years and every one of them says 'armed and dangerous'. One of us will have to sit guard at night."

They rode into a stand of cottonwood trees along the almost dry river, found a fair patch of grass for the animals, and stopped for the night. Messing untied the two outlaws and was about to pull Kimble from his horse when Waco Bob spurred his horse and bolted from camp. He had spent the day working the ropes until they just hung limp as they rode into camp. He threw the rope free as he raced away.

Betsy had just stepped off her horse when Waco Bob made his getaway and was

knocked down by the outlaw's horse. She fell hard into a pile of rocks and was knocked unconscious.

Corcoran jumped on Rube and had his big horse in a full gallop in half a stride. The chase along the dried bed of the river, up the bank and back down through stands of trees, and out on the desert plain was fast and furious.

Waco Bob was an excellent rider as was Corcoran; they both rode fine horses that could run for long periods and Corcoran worried if he would catch Torres. "Come on, Rube boy, give it everything you've got," he urged, jumping a dead-fall of cottonwood. Waco Bob turned to go back down into the riverbed when his horse stumbled in loose sand, sending the outlaw face first down the embankment.

Corcoran leapt off Rube, crashing into Waco Bob, the two rolling in the mud and wet sand. Torres was tough but was hurt in the fall and Corcoran smashed him in the face three times before pulling the heavy Colt and shoving the barrel into the outlaw's mouth. "Just one little twitch, Torres. Just one. You don't know how much I want you dead right now."

It was a slow ride back to the campsite with Torres walking his limping horse and Corcoran telling the man over and over just how stupid he was and how much he wished he would make another escape attempt. "Come on, stupid, try it. Go on, you coward, run for it," he hollered over and over. Waco Bob Torres wasn't quite that stupid. They found a good fire burning and everyone huddled around Betsy when they rode into camp.

Corcoran walked Torres to where Kimble was tied up, slammed his rifle barrel across the man's head, knocking him out cold. He tied his hands behind his back and in turn tied the long lasso around the tree the two outlaws were sitting under. Corcoran looked at Kimble, indicated the rifle, and said, "One little move and you both die."

Doherty rushed over and grabbed Corcoran. "Hurry man, Betsy's hurt bad." The big Irisher ran to the fire and knelt down next to the lovely lady. Her head was wrapped in bloody rags and he could see scrapes and cuts all across her face.

"She was knocked down face first into the rocks, Corcoran. She hasn't woke up since." Nate Coppersmith was sitting in the dirt and had Betsy's head in his lap, wiping her face with a damp cloth. "She took a horrible fall."

Corcoran's first thought was to grab her up in his arms and hold her as tight as he could but knew that would do even more damage to the girl. Then he wanted to walk over and shoot Waco Bob Torres fifty times or more, and knew he couldn't do that either. Instead, Corcoran sat down next to Nate and took one of Betsy's hands in his, rubbing it gently and telling her he was there.

He eased Nate Copperfield aside and held Betsy's head in his lap, talking to her in a voice so low and gentle no one else could understand him. "I'll take care of you, Betsy, for the rest of my life. I've been talking to myself about us, you know. I've told Rube several times that I think I'm in love for the first time in my life.

"I don't know nothing about cows but I do know about horses. I doubt I could build a house but I'm willing to try. I've never worked a plow or built an irrigation ditch but I bet I could."

He spent the entire night talking to his Shaggy Hair and was sound asleep with her head in his lap when Seamus Doherty got the morning fire going and coffee boiling. Betsy

Schultz had not wakened once during the night. Camp was busy, breakfast was quick, animals were saddled and packed, and Betsy hadn't wakened.

"We need a travois," Corcoran said. "Connect it to Rube, he's been there before, and I'll walk alongside. Don't let Torres ride that horse. If the limp gets worse, it would probably mean a broken leg and we'll have to put it down. That goes for Torres, too." The comment might have been slightly humorous but it also carried a direct threat that everyone understood.

It was late morning before the caravan got underway with Corcoran leading Rube and the rest well out in front. Rube simply followed along and Corcoran walked alongside the travois talking to Betsy the whole time. She never opened her eyes, never twitched, never moved the entire day. He spent a great amount of time looking into her peaceful face, noticing her even breathing.

He whispered so many times, "I love you, Shaggy Hair," hoping she would respond but there was never so much as a twitch. He felt more helpless that he had ever felt; had anger and rage boiling his blood; wanted to kill Waco Bob fifty times and hold his Shaggy Hair for a hundred and fifty years. What continued to bother him was the senselessness of the accident.

When they stopped for a mid-day meal, Corcoran wiped her face with cool water, squeezed some into her mouth, and got no reaction.

"She's gonna die, Seamus," Corcoran said, sitting next to the travois, holding her hand. Doherty saw tears running down his friend's face. They had flowed for most of the morning, he thought, judging by the tracks through the dust and grime of the trail. "I found what you said I should find, Seamus."

Doherty couldn't find any words that would work, just

stood alongside his friend, quietly crying with him. Corcoran had Rube in the shade of a large lightning-wracked cottonwood tree and sat quietly next to his Shaggy Hair. Betsy passed over within the hour and Corcoran dug the grave, not allowing anyone near him or her.

He brought water from the almost dry creek called a river and washed Betsy's face clean, wrapped her in his bedroll and placed her gently in the deep, sandy grave. "I'm not much on church doins," he said, his deep voice so gentle and soft most couldn't hear him. "I'll just say goodbye, dear lady, and ask that your travels now be safe and warm."

He sat next to the grave for the rest of the day, telling Messing and Doherty to go on without him. "I'm riding north to Grant County. Her father needs to know. Don't let Torres get away. Charge him with her death." His eyes were red, his mouth drawn down severely, and his body wracked with sobs as he watched them ride off toward Winnemucca. He spent hours telling Betsy stories, sang her a song or two, remembered poetry from his father and uncles, and finally undid the travois and mounted Rube for the long ride into whatever future he might have. His parting words were simple.

"I love you, Shaggy Hair."

It was a long slow ride north to Dave Schultz's home and a long sad visit with Betsy's father. "I had made up my mind, Dave. I was going to give up the badge, quit the long trail, and it was a bad man, an outlaw who changed my mind. I don't know if I could have made it as a husband, father, rancher. The first time some bastard did something, I'd look for that badge."

"Maybe," Schultz said. "I lost my wife and ranch and took up the law because of it. Maybe we're fighting those old windmills, Corcoran. Betsy was one of a kind as far as my life goes and I can see in your eyes she was the only one for you. You have a law-dog's fire and maybe this is a little over the top, but outlaws should tremble at hearing your name."

Corcoran left Oregon and rode to the Seamus Doherty spread in Paradise Valley to spend a few days with his old friend. "Few men have lost what you've lost, Terrence," Doherty said. "Don't pin that badge on, nail it tight. Don't ever let any man take it from you."

Doherty was sitting in front of his fire nursing a hot brandy watching Corcoran pace around the room. He was chuckling as he contemplated a thought or two. "You would have been a disaster as a rancher, Corcoran, and, damn me, I can't imagine how you would have raised children but I know for a fact that you would have been happy. I'm so very sorry for your loss.

"Go home now, back to Eureka, nail that badge to your chest and put fear in the hearts of outlaws everywhere."

It was a month before Corcoran rode into Winnemucca and tied his horse off in front of the sheriff's office. "Glad you're here, Corcoran. You okay?"

"Yup. Coffee hot?"

"It is. Torres will be off on the morning train to Carson City. Life with no parole. Tried my best to get him hung but the judge wouldn't buy it."

"He'll suffer some. Maybe they'll let him out down the line. I'd like that."

Messing gave him a strange look and Corcoran continued. "Well, if he's out, he'll always be a bastard and I'll chase him down and kill him good. I'll kill him three times or more."

"That's better," Messing said. He walked to the stove and brought the coffee pot over. "If you want help on that, you know where to find me," he chuckled.

"How about Nate?"

"Federal judge gave him his homestead claim back. Bunch of trials coming up sometime in the spring. I guess we'll all get called on that. What about you, Corcoran? Plans?"

"Sent a wire to my boss in Eureka," Corcoran said, a slight grin creeping across his face. "Said if I'm not back in ten days wearing my badge, he's sending a posse out. Guess my vacation is over. Don't think I'll take another one. Ever." He took a long draught of hot coffee and sat down in an old bent cane chair. "Sheriff said there's all kinds of trouble brewing and I need to hustle."

"I got a wire, too," Messing said, rummaging around the desktop clutter. "From the sheriff in Salt Lake City. Says that Bronco Johnny Ladd broke free and was last seen riding west. Isn't he the one has a price on your head?"

"Yup," Corcoran sighed. "Bronco Johnny comin' this way, eh? I've wanted to put him down for a long time." He drank the coffee Messing poured and headed for the office door. "Get down Eureka way, you got a couple of beers comin', Sam Messing."

"Hasta la vista, amigo. Stay warm."

"I wonder if the trouble coming toward Eureka is Bronco Johnny? Now that would just about put a capper on this so-called vacation of mine." Corcoran was talking to himself all the way down the broad stairs of the courthouse.

Messing almost choked on his coffee as he watched the lanky Corcoran walk out the door and pull his old sombrero down on his head. Attached to the back of the hatband was a thatch of blonde, wiry, shaggy hair, tied with a pink ribbon. "When he fell, he fell hard. I hope that old boy don't go into some kind of damned tailspin."

"All right, Rube, let's get it on. From now on, it's you and me down here and that beautiful Shaggy Hair up there keeping watch over us. Let's go home, big boy."

A LOOK AT EZEKIEL'S JOURNEY BY JOHNNY GUNN

His life is shattered, his wife, his children dead. A lesser man might just give it up; but Ezekiel Hawthorne isn't a quitter. While thousands head to the California gold fields in wagons, Ezekiel loads his mule and embarks on an amazing venture across the continent alone, bound for the good soils and abundant waters of Oregon. Savages, tornadoes, and a lack of knowledge don't slow the man down a bit. It's a beautiful half-Shoshone woman who has the biggest impact on Ezekiel's new life.

AVAILABLE NOW ON AMAZON

ABOUT THE AUTHOR

Reno, Nevada novelist, Johnny Gunn, is retired from a long career in journalism. He has worked in print, broadcast, and Internet, including a stint as publisher and editor of the Virginia City Legend. These days, Gunn spends most of his time writing novel length fiction, concentrating on the western genre. Or, you can find him down by the Truckee River with a fly rod in hand.

"it's been a wonderful life. I was born in Santa Cruz, California, on the north shore of fabled Monterey Bay. When I was fourteen, that would have been 1953, we moved to Guam and I went through my high school years living in a tropical paradise. I learned to scuba dive from a WWII Navy Frogman, learned to fly from a WWII combat pilot (by dad), but I knew how to fish long before I moved to Guam.

"I spent time on the Island of Truk, which during WWII was a huge Japanese naval base, and dived in the lagoon. Massive U.S. air strikes sunk thousands of tons of Japanese naval craft, and it was more than exciting to dive on those wrecks. In the Palau Islands, near Koror, I also dived on Japanese aircraft that had been shot down into the lagoons.

Made in the USA
Las Vegas, NV
25 March 2023

69656414R00135